The Floating World – the Madelyn Chapters

by A.A.Cain

Published by: A.A.Cain,

PO Box 117, Campbelltown, South Australia, 5074.

Email: writingbyaacain.gmail.com

First Edition: 2019

ISBN:

epub   978-0-9876330-1-9

print   978-0-9876330-6-4

Printed and distributed by Lulu.com

Contents

Madelyn in the Street

As she went down in the lift Madelyn unzipped the bottom ten inches of her tight leather skirt, nearly revealing the top of a fine silk stocking on her left thigh, but not quite.

Around the office she made sure the zip was always fully done up, that dramatic slash from the right side of her waist to the bottom left of the skirt, zipped closed. The cling of the skirt was tight, so her steps were kept short, one foot in front of the other, and her hips rocked when she was in the office.

She played it, the discreetly sexual up and coming corporate executive, for all it was worth. It was part of Maddy's tool box, and even though the office notice boards were full of gender equity workshops and aspirational targets, she knew that was all bullshit. If the men in the office speculated whether she wore a bra or not, with her slender torso and perfectly tailored blouses and jackets in winter; or delighted in the pale blue or purple or sometimes even pink bra straps, thin and delicate, with her sleeveless tops in summer, so be it.

Maddy was tall and elegant, and looked good in whatever she chose to wear, so why not wear it? All the men did, those who could, anyway, those who could still wear a well-tailored suit and hold their gut in. A decidedly shrinking group of men, as the years passed them by, but those who could, did, and so did Maddy. Playing them at their own game, she actually played it better, because she knew exactly what made them look. And Maddy? She looked right back and challenged the men. As a consequence she was mostly left alone, and preferred it that way.

Because she was tall and her legs were long, and longer still in her five inch Louboutin heels, Maddy needed the freedom of the undone zip to allow her to stride, once she got outside. She was one of those rare women who actually knew how to walk in heels, and that got her noticed, too. Red soles on the pavement - sometimes that was the only bright colour she wore - flashes of red as she walked.

She swept swiftly from the building's lobby out to a wide pavement, but her forward surge was interrupted by a pair of slow suits dawdling in front of her, phones in their hands, their fat asses in her way. She shook her head, *get out of my way,* and swerved off to the right, her heels clicking fast on the concrete pavement. As she walked past the two men she glanced across, and there on the other side of the pair was a tall man, matching her pace, he too frustrated by the slow movement of the duo between them. She caught his eye, and there it was, a conspiratorial smile, glancing across at her.

Maddy smiled back, holding his gaze, and when they were both sufficiently far in front of the crawling pair they both swerved in towards each other, matching their long paces until they walked side by side.

"Don't you hate it when people dawdle in front of you?" he commented. "Getting in your way."

She laughed. "God, yes. I haven't got all day!"

She looked directly at him, for in her heels Maddy matched his height, even had an inch or two on him. She quickly took in his short, silvering hair, close cropped beard, and his dark charcoal suit, no tie. An elegant man, fast walking, whose eyes had glanced over her.

Five metres on they came to a road, and he punched the button for the walk sign. "I don't know why I do that. It's on its own cycle."

She laughed. "Maybe you get special privileges, being in a hurry, knowing what you want."

"Yes, maybe. But it wasn't red, I wouldn't get to talk to you."

"Stop pushing the button, then." She looked at him with her wide open gaze, and decided she liked this man. She touched his arm. "We can wait."

"What shall we talk about, while we wait?" he asked, his deep blue eyes holding hers.

"Oh, this and that. It's a lovely day, the weather's perfect. Oh look, there's the walk sign, shall we cross? Are you walking the next block? We can walk together."

"That would be nice, yes. The next block."

They crossed the road, side by side, their shoulders almost touching, almost brushing where her fingers had been. A short way down the block Maddy suddenly stopped, and he stopped too. She put out her hand to shake his in a greeting. "Hi. I'm Maddy. It's lovely to meet you."

"Hello Maddy," he replied. "Lovely to meet you, too. I'm Adam."

"Hello Adam. There, that's the formalities, done." She grinned at him, and started walking. "Well, are you coming?"

He smiled back at her, and caught up. She momentarily wondered if he could be told. Told what to do.

Then it was Adam's turn to stop. "This is my building, I go in here." He pointed to the lobby with its eight lifts, four each side.

"Oh, that's a shame. I was hoping we could walk together a bit longer." She touched his arm again. Then, on a whim, and because he might be a man who might have one, she asked, "Do you have a business card on you?"

He did, in a fine silver case kept in an inside pocket of his jacket. He passed a card to her. She turned it over in her hand, running a fingertip along the embossed lettering.

"Adam Cain," she read, "Strategic Projects Consultant. Ah ha, is that what you are? Thanks."

"May I have your number?" he asked.

"Oh no, Mister Cain, I don't do that." She leaned forward and quickly kissed him on the cheek. "I shall call you," said Madelyn, "when I choose." She blew him another kiss. "When I need a Strategic Projects Consultant." She winked, and he laughed.

She walked on and didn't look back. She knew he would keep watching as she continued down the block, until she was out of sight.

Madelyn saw Adam several times over the next weeks, always from a distance, his movements loosely coinciding with hers, but not fully in her orbit, not yet.

She saw him dance with a slim girl coming out of the cafe next to his building, after the girl had rushed from the door and nearly collided with him, walking by. He spun her in his arms to stop her from falling, then they walked together down the block. Maddy smiled as he jabbed the Walk button, *I don't know why I do that.* She smiled again as the girl took a step back, slung a hand on her hip, and studied the man. What the girl saw must have pleased her, for when they crossed the road she put her arm inside Adam's and looked up at him. They were familiar with each other, that was obvious.

Another time, several weeks later, Maddy saw Adam exit the same cafe, to be followed moments later by a slender boy with a hip bag and long glossy hair, who ran to catch up with Adam at the same crossing. They clearly spoke to each other, for when the lights changed they crossed, side by side.

Maddy wondered, in another whim of curiosity, if Adam's daytime existence was somehow defined by this one city block and its boundary of roads and controlled crossings. She pondered too the unlikely odds that his excursions coincided with her own. She decided to find out. Her work provided an excuse, so she called him from her office.

"Hi, Mr Cain, Adam? You might remember me? Maddy, we met in the street, and you gave me your card."

   ...

"Yes, that's right, the tall girl who walked fast. At the crossing,"

   ...

"Of course I remember. Listen, I work for _____ and was wondering if you..."

Maddy described a brief assignment a project team needed to get done, that seemed to fit within the portfolio of work described on the Cain website, which she had quickly checked. "Is that something you do?"

   ...

"It is? Perfect. When can we meet?"

   ...

"You'll come here? Wonderful."

Meeting Adam

Maddy set up a time and gave Adam her building's address and instructions to meet her in the lobby. She then booked Meeting Space Three, one of the "new flexible working arrangements, to increase your comfort and our productivity." In reality, MS3 was a pair of intimate meeting cocoons, like huge eggs, facing each other in a quiet corner of the building, with clear views looking out over a broad city square. The seats could be swivelled to look outwards or inwards, "to meet the needs of every participant." Maddy thought it was mostly all rubbish and architectural pretension, but the pods made a change from the noise of the open plan workspaces and got her on to a different floor for an hour. Sometimes she got tired of their eyes, their faceless eyes, and would walk away.

What the meeting space arrangements did bring, with management insisting on it stridently, was a policy of absolute privacy. *Our business requires confidentiality at all times. When a meeting is underway, respect our client's needs always, and do not ever interrupt.*

Maddy found the privacy rules very convenient some lunchtimes, and would book her favourite space, MS3, and turn both pods to face outside. She'd curl up in one pod, completely hidden from those inside the office, tuck one leg under her bottom, undo the zip most of its length, and dip her fingers deep inside her wet sex. Rainy days were best, the rain lashing in sheets against the glass, and the background wash of noise meant she could cry out softly when she came.

She met Adam downstairs in the lobby and signed him in. He was wearing a dark charcoal suit, a shade he clearly favoured, with a deep blue shirt and silk tie. He dresses for his eyes, she thought, and absorbed his gaze, not looking away. The only embellishment he wore was a slim silver watch on his right wrist, its dial facing outwards.

"You're not wearing a purple shirt," she remarked, ushering him into the lift.

"Purple shirt?" he asked.

"Don't all consultants wear purple shirts?" she replied, her voice straight but her eyes creased in a smile. "With a white collar, to signify the bonus?"

"Ah, you know the breed." Adam smiled in response, still holding her gaze. "But no. I don't own a purple shirt. Even the tie I don't like, I prefer not wearing ties." He shook his head.

"Did you wear the tie on my account?" Maddy asked. "You shouldn't have. Be comfortable, take it off."

"I will, thanks." He quickly unlooped the tie and pulled it from around his neck, undoing the top button of his shirt. "Ah that's better. I can breathe." He coiled the tie and placed it in his jacket pocket.

"Yes, be relaxed." Maddy deliberately undid the top buttons of her blouse, two below her throat, and teased the collar apart to reveal the top of her chest, her pale alabaster skin. She reached over to Adam and deftly undid the next button down on his shirt, exposing a hint of greying hair on his chest. "There. Much better."

All the while she watched his reaction during her little ceremony, as if it were a test. He barely blinked. She didn't make him nervous, that was good. Maddy didn't trust nervous men.

Maddy enjoyed this man. They swiftly covered the project brief, its objectives, agreed rates and terms, and she appreciated his fast intelligence, keeping up with hers. After half an hour she went and made two coffees from the self-brew machine in the kitchen, and brought them back, signifying an end to the business side of the meeting. She was relaxed anyway, but wanted to enjoy more time with Adam.

When she leaned forward to hand him the coffee she knew, if her angle was just right, there'd be a perfect gap in the fall of her blouse, revealing a glimpse of a tight conical breast with a soft puffed nipple, dark pink. She watched his face as Adam took the coffee, and saw his pupils dilate, seeing her perfect angle, just right.

"Thank you," he said softly, and she leaned forward a little more to hear his low voice.

"My pleasure," she replied, her voice low, too. "I hope it's hot enough."

Adam took a sip and looked back at her. "Ah yes, perfect."

Maddy took her own seat, tucking a leg under her bottom in her favourite lunchtime position.

"Do you mind if I'm more comfortable? This skirt...." She unzipped two-thirds of the zip, revealing the top of her stockings and the pale flesh of her thighs. "Ahh, that's better." She eased her long thighs comfortably apart, revealing a shadow and a hint of her sex.

"More perfection?" Adam carefully asked, with a glint of pleasure in his eyes.

"Oh, yes, don't you think so?"

Maddy eased her body back further, relaxing even more into the comfort of the pod and the caress of his eyes. The hem of her skirt crept higher, revealing a longer hint of her sex and a creamy shadow between her thighs.

Adam watched as Madelyn exhibited herself before him, her fingers slow in her cunt as she came. She looked at him watching her, closing her eyes only in the final shuddering quiver of her orgasm.

"I'm not going to get your personal number, am I?" Adam asked.

"Oh no, Mister Cain, I don't do that. But can I have your tie?"

Madelyn saw Adam several times over the course of the project, but denied herself the delight of displaying herself to him again. By denying herself she denied Adam too, and over time she sensed a frustration in him. She imagined him reliving the sight of her slow moving fingers deep in her sex, and wondered if he came, thinking of her. She had no idea if Adam had a partner or partners, and didn't care. She was only interested in her own pleasure, and if tormenting him was an adjunct to that, so be it.

Yet she delighted in the man, his generous approach to the project team as he recounted examples and anecdotes from his career, stories from the men and women who had mentored and taught him professionally. And over time, seeing this side of Adam, Maddy began to wonder about the men and women who had made him the man he was in his private life. She thought mostly women, but was never quite sure.

She decided she wanted to know more. So she called him from the office, just before leaving work one day, early in the week.

"Adam, hi, it's Maddy."

...

"Can I buy you dinner? Yes? When suits?"

...

"Thursday evening, yes. Give me your address, I'll pick you up."

...

"Okay, I know it. Outside, at seven?"

Maddy hung up the phone, smiling. She'd look forward to a meal with Adam very much indeed. She pondered what to wear... ah yes, that dress would be.perfect.

The Restaurant

Maddy parked outside Adam's apartment a few minutes before seven, just to see how punctual he would be. His work discipline was to the minute; she was intrigued to see if that precision carried over socially.

Two minutes later he leaned over the convertible's passenger side door and greeted her.

"I came down as soon as I saw a car and recognised the driver. It's a slow old lift, you have to wait, I'm afraid." He smiled, and tapped the clock in the centre of the dash. "You were early, though. See, I'm right on time." The minute hand was on the twelve.

Maddy looked up at him with a cheeky glint in her eyes. "I was testing you."

"I thought you might be. Did I pass?"

"Oh yes, I think so." As Adam got into the car, Maddy noticed his right wrist was bare. "But you don't have your watch."

"I don't keep time outside work. Time's my own, when it's mine."

She started the car, her thigh tightening as she pushed down the clutch, the long flow of her dark green dress carefully bunched behind her legs, out of the way.

"So it takes as long as it takes," she said, "whatever it is that you do." It wasn't a question, more an observation, even a statement of fact.

"Something like that. Why, do you have a deadline?"

"Midnight, Mister Cain, you'll find a glass slipper and a girl on the run."

"Mice and a pumpkin, too?"

"Something like that."

Maddy put a stop to the back and forth. She'd tested him, but wasn't quite sure what it told her. With a twitch in her jaw, she leaned over and kissed him on the cheek, marking him with her lipstick, a deep red. Adam touched a finger to the spot she'd kissed, and saw the colour on his fingertip. She looked at him with her certain eyes, and smiled, more to herself. She'd marked him first.

"Wear your watch, next time," she said.

Maddy shook her head to clear hair from her cheek. "I want to drive fast for a while, so I've booked a place in the hills."

She pulled her russet red hair back, slipping a band around it to keep it off her face. She flicked the car into gear, looked back over her right shoulder, and neatly accelerated into the light traffic.

Maddy enjoyed driving, the crisp snick of the box as she ranged up and down the gears, the bark of the engine when she used it to brake. In the city she drove with her palm resting on the gear knob, to be instantly ready to shift, with her right hand at two o'clock on the wheel. She didn't want Adam to talk as she concentrated in the traffic, and he didn't. She glanced across at him from time to time, and he seemed comfortable enough in her hands, his right hand resting on his knee; deliberately so, she thought, to be near her gear changing hand.

Hitting the freeway, Maddy flicked the car into fourth, then fifth and set cruise at one-hundred-and-ten. She dropped her gear hand onto Adam's resting hand, picked it up, and placed it on her thigh. A crass man would shift his hand to her crotch, but Maddy knew Adam wouldn't do that. She rested her left hand on top of his for a moment, gave it a squeeze, then placed both hands on the steering wheel. The wind was fast in her face.

Maddy flicked back to fourth, accelerating to pass a semi on a hill, and Adam shifted his hand back to his own knee. She smiled. She drove well, so he got out of her way and let her drive.

After fifteen minutes driving fast on the freeway, colour high on her cheeks from the wind, Maddy pulled off into a truck stop, deserted this early in the evening, its long concrete slabs lit by five lights on tall poles. She pulled up and parked in a circle of light.

"I need a pee. Come on, hold up my dress."

She got out of the car and crouched down, facing the rear quarter of the vehicle, her back to the road. She bunched the dress up in a mess about her waist, revealing her long stocking clad legs and a garter belt, no panties. Coming around the back of the car, Adam caught a glimpse of her belly, a dash of red darkness at its base.

"Quickly," she said, handing him a fold of her dress. "Keep it off the ground."

Adam leaned back against the car and Maddy tilted forward, placing both hands on his hips for balance, her head down to see herself. She relaxed, and let go with a sigh of pleasure, "Ahh, that's good." Her flow of piss jetted and splashed on the ground, running down in a stream towards the car, circling Adam's shoes, marking him with her scent. He didn't move his feet away, and breathed in the faint acrid smell of her piss.

Maddy looked up into Adam's face gazing down at her, a slight wonder in his eyes. She quivered with the pleasure of her release, and squeezed out a last small trickle.

"I needed to go," she said, as if that was a perfectly naturally explanation for her action.

She moved one hand to cover his cock. He wasn't hard, but thickened under the weight of her touch. Still looking up at him, she undid his belt buckle, the button at his waist band, and pulled down the zip. She pressed against his hardening flesh, still looking up into his eyes.

She dipped a finger between her legs and flavoured herself with her urine, then reached up to Adam's lips to scent him too. His cock throbbed as he took her finger into his mouth and sucked, looking down at her. Maddy looked away, and dipped her hand into his briefs, holding the hot weight of his balls for a moment, before extracting the long hard length of him from his pants. She pushed him back against the car for stability, then took his plum coloured head into her mouth, cupping her hand up against his balls again, pulling them towards her.

Maddy took Adam into her throat, her gag reflex stopped, her suck tight around his shaft. He was fully hard now, and she discovered his length and took his measure. Her mouth was a slow suck, and she felt a gentle hand on her head, then both hands in her hair. She dipped between her legs once more, and teased up her clit, stroking it and pressing. She took her own pleasure first. Sucking Adam's cock was part of her luxury, it wasn't for him.

A truck sped by on the free-way, its driver giving them a blast on the horn as it passed.

Madelyn took her own fast pleasure and came, her fingers dipped in her cunt. She backed away from Adam, leaving him thick and hard, his shaft glistening with her suckling spit, marked red with her dark lipstick. She stood up, put her cunt wet fingers to his mouth, and kissed him hard, savouring her taste mixed with his. She breathed deeply, taking the rising musky smell of him into her nose, breathing him in.

"Put yourself away, Mister Cain. I'm hungry, and the booking's for eight. We mustn't be late." She carefully took Adam's length and placed it sideways in his pants. "Oh dear, you're hard, what shall we do?"

"Fuck, you bitch," Adam muttered.

"Oh my," Madelyn said. "Is that control, or losing it?"

"I thought..."

"Ah, there's the thing. Don't think. It's like your Walk button, you don't need to push it."

Maddy looked at him, and took pity. "Look at me, Adam, in this dress. What do you think I've got on, underneath?"

She took a step back, spread her arms wide, and the dress clung to every tight curve above her waist, flowing over her hips like water. It was cut in a long vee to her navel, revealing the smooth curves of her small breasts and bare shoulders.

"Not much," Adam agreed.

"Nothing at all, in fact. My stockings and a garter belt, nothing else." She caressed his cheek, and came forward to kiss his mouth. "Don't be so impatient, Mister Cain. What Madelyn promises, Madelyn delivers; you should know me well enough by now, to know that?"

She reached into the car for her bag and pulled out a tissue. Dabbing it to her tongue for moisture, she carefully removed the earlier touch of lipstick from Adam's cheek.

"There. My lipstick's still on your skin, but the restaurant doesn't need to know where." She looked at him with bright eyes, and ran her finger down his cheek to his chin, turning his face directly to hers.

"Mister Cain, I think I'm going to enjoy you, very much. But you mustn't be so... forward. Is that the right word? Forward? Fast?"

She was playing with him, and the creases around his eyes told Maddy he knew that. "Get in the car, you silly boy. I'm hungry, let's eat."

"What Madelyn wants, Madelyn gets, is that it," he asked, adjusting his softening but still full cock in his pants, then doing up his belt.

"Something like that. When I want it," she replied, sliding into the driver's seat and closing the door with a satisfying thunk. She started the engine, waiting for Adam to click on his seat belt. "You may place your hand on my leg, if you like," she said.

"What if I don't want to?"

"Then you're a liar."

Maddy liked the soft weight of his hand and its movement on her thigh every time she changed gear. She left the freeway. The road curved tightly up and down hills, and she drove quickly, running up and down through the gears. He didn't move his hand away, not this time.

When they arrived at the restaurant, Maddy pulled a small pair of knickers from her bag, and slipped them on, shimmying down the dress so it flowed over her slender figure like water.

"I need something with soft cotton," she said, "so I don't mark the chair."

They stepped into the restaurant, side by side, and the maître-de hurried up to them.

"I have a booking," Madelyn said.

"Certainly, Madame, what name?"

"Oh please, you're mistaken. Mademoiselle, surely." Her eyes were gleeful as she corrected him. "Madelyn, it will be under Madelyn."

"Of course, Miss Madelyn, let me check... here we are, for two. Please, follow me."

"Oh dear," she stage whispered to Adam. "Miss Madelyn. Am I really so obvious?"

"Not on the phone, Maddy, I wouldn't have thought so." Adam replied.

"Oh, you delicious man. Always saying the right thing."

"One learns, Madelyn."

"I hope so, Mister Cain. I certainly hope so." She looked at him, her eyes sparkling.

The temperature in the restaurant rose as Maddy moved past the other patrons, dragging their eyes away from their partners like smoke rising from a flame. Adam followed behind, enjoying the cling of her dress against the line of her thighs and her delectable ass. Arriving at their table, the maître-de pulled out the chair for Madelyn and she sat, gracefully swinging her long legs away from the aisle. With a quick flourish, he spread the napkin across her lap. The flow of her dress was split high on her thigh, so the maître-de carefully looked at the top of her head.

"Mademoiselle."

"Thank you so much. What should I call you? Your name, I mean."

"Jean-Claude, M'amselle."

She looked up at him, with an eyebrow raised. "Are you sure?"

"John, really. It's just John."

She smiled. "Melbourne, not Paris?"

"You've caught me, Miss. Footscray, actually."

"Well, just John from Footscray. Let's see if the chef lives up to *his* name, shall we?"

The maître-de turned to Adam. "I'm sorry, sir, leaving you standing. May I assist?"

"Thank you, Jean-Claude."

Adam took the arms of the chair and in one smooth move, made himself comfortable. The napkin was swiftly placed on his lap, and the maître-de quickly retired.

"Was that necessary?" Adam asked Madelyn.

She gazed at him, not blinking, then touched a knife that was perfectly aligned on the table with the tip of her finger.

"Not really," she acknowledged. A tiny thrill touched the pit of her belly. Was Adam going to challenge her?

Adam touched his finger to his own knife, it too perfectly aligned on the table. "You shouldn't, not when they can't get away. It's too easy."

"Whereas you, Mister Cain, came willingly?"

"Madelyn, with you, I suspect I won't come at all."

A number of patrons looked across to their table, hearing the pure joy of Maddy's laugh. The low murmur of the restaurant resumed. Outside, the shapes of trees shifting in a low breeze interrupted the flicker of lights from the city on the plain below, and the night grew dark around them.

A waitress, warned no doubt by Jean-Claude, came to take their order. She stood by Adam's chair, for protection perhaps, or to better read Maddy's face as she gave her order. Maddy watched the girl walk away.

"You do that, don't you? A lot," she observed.

"What do I do?" Adam asked.

"Pay them undivided attention, your women. That waitress. You made her feel special. Just for that minute, she was the only woman in the room. Most men don't do that. Most men don't know how."

Adam smiled. "You're not the first to say that. I didn't know what it meant at first, but yes, I do that. It comes naturally to me, I think."

"I'm sure it does," Maddy replied. "You appreciate women, and let them know. I like that in a man."

She looked at him with her steady eyes. "I like your attention, Adam. A lot. It's rare, for me, to want something that I can't just take from a man." She took a sip of water. "You intrigue me, Adam Cain. Very much."

She glanced up to see the maître-de coming to take their drinks order. "Should I be kind to him? Apologise?" Maddy's eyes were cold as she said it, but it was no cost to her to pretend.

"You should, yes."

"Jean-Claude, I was very rude before. I'm sorry." She touched her fingers to Jean-Claude's wrist, just under the cuff of his sleeve. She gently brushed his skin, looking up at him with her dark eyes, the angle of her shallow cleavage just right for his look.

"Mademoiselle, it was nothing."

Her pale nipple appeased him for a moment as he took their wine order, then Maddy sat back and took her body away from his eyes. Under the table, she stretched out a leg to reach Adam's calf. Still thick from her earlier suck, he eased his thighs apart.

"I only did that for you," she said.

"I know. But thank you, anyway."

With a wave of her hand she dismissed the topic. The maître-de was of no interest to her.

"So, Adam, tell me about yourself. What kind of a man are you?"

"I could ask you that, Maddy. I'm the kind of man you take to dinner after a ride in your fast car, given head by the side of the road. What kind of a man is that? Surely you can tell me?"

"*Touché*, Mister Cain."

With her own instinctive ability, Maddy let Adam talk. She listened to his low, vaguely English accented voice wander from this topic to that, and she saw again the generosity he'd given her project team, a nurturing care for people that seemed to come naturally to him.

She wondered about that, knowing she didn't have that quality in herself, and was curious. She knew he was kind, and she was not. Maddy didn't much care about people, other than what they could do for her, yet this man intrigued her.

What quality in her did he want? He could have said no to dinner, refused her mouth on his cock, refused her slit cunt before his eyes in the office when she'd called him. Was that it, Maddy thought, that she'd called him? Adam seemed quite content to be at her call, but surely it wasn't that simple?

"Maddy? Are you there?" Adam's fingers touched hers. "You've wandered off."

"I'm sorry, Adam. I was wondering..."

"Wondering what, Maddy? What kind of a man I am?"

"Not quite." She looked at him, and surprised herself with her answer. "I was wondering what kind of a woman I am. Which is odd, because I thought I knew."

"Don't doubt yourself, Madelyn. Not now. You don't do that, remember."

She recovered herself, but remained uncertain. "Would you excuse me for a moment? I'll be right back."

She walked through the restaurant, once again followed by admiring and envious eyes, both men and women watching her feline grace. She hoped Adam was watching too, but he couldn't easily be read, and that unsettled her. Was she in control, or losing it?

In the women's restroom, Maddy entered a toilet cubicle and sat down on the lid. She pulled the length of her dress up to her lap, bunching the silk there. She tugged the morsel of knickers down her legs, and brought them up to her nose. She breathed in her own aroma, inhaling it deeply, the faint waft of her earlier unwiped pee, the slightly tart smell of her earlier arousal.

It wasn't enough. She needed herself more, to remove her momentary doubt. Placing the panties in her bag, Maddy spread her right leg wide until her knee rested hard against the wall of the cubicle. She slipped her other shoe off, and lifted her long leg up so she could push hard against the door, giving herself easy access to her sex.

Maddy wanted her cunt to ache, and she realised that's what was missing. Her mouth, her lips, they'd been stretched by Adam's cock and her deep suck, but her cunt was empty, unfilled except by her own long fingers.

Fuck, she thought, *I don't want him just for that, surely not*? Angry with herself for wanting something so basic, so crude, from a man, she wet two fingers and dipped them to her sex, spreading wide the top of her lips to find the shaft of her clitoris, to bring it up from its hidden place and to give herself quick pleasure, to satisfy herself; no man needed for that.

She knew her climax could be fast, but soon lost her sense of time. As she dipped her fingers, Maddy allowed herself to slow, to envelope herself in pleasure. She tasted her arousal, moving her fingers back and forth from her mouth, lipstick messy and her fingers tipped with red, back to her cunt where she dipped and felt her own slick juice. She tasted herself and took her own pleasure, forgetting about time. Her thigh muscles ached from the hard push back, and her knee knocked against the cubicle wall.

Dimly, she registered a door opening, and she froze, licking wetness from her fingers. She touched the wet fingers to her neck, and felt a hot heat there. *Fuuck, so close.*

"Madame, are you all right?"

Maddy recognised the voice of the waitress. Adam must have become concerned and asked the girl to check. She looked down and saw a shadow on the floor. The girl was right outside her cubicle door, very close.

So close. Maddy decided. "A tip," she said. "Two hundred dollars if you come in here."

There was no reply, but Maddy heard a sharp intake of breath. "It's not drugs," she clarified. "Sex. I need fingers to fuck me. That's all. Two minutes. Not long."

There was a long silence, and another intake of breath. "Three hundred," the girl replied. "Three hundred, and nothing said. I don't get fired for this, not fucking fired."

"Not fired." Maddy agreed. "Nothing said. Three hundred bucks."

She leaned forward to unlatch the lock, then sat back on the toilet lid, her thighs spread wide, her dress bunched about her waist, falling long to the floor. The cubicle door opened slowly, and the waitress came in, not knowing what to expect, not knowing what she'd see. Her eyes opened wide as she saw Maddy's dishevelled state, her wide open legs.

The girl took another deep breath. "How... what do you want me to do?"

She looked down at Madelyn sprawled cunt naked, legs spread wide before her. She saw the mess of lipstick on Maddy's mouth and on her fingers, and could smell the woman. The girl rubbed her hands nervously together, not sure what the other woman wanted, not sure what she was doing.

"Your fingers. Two, three, however you fuck with fingers. Fast inside me. Just a fuck." Maddy knew she was close, just needing this wrongness to finish her off. "Kiss me, will you kiss me? Your tongue a fuck?"

"You're a crazy bitch. Fucking hell! Cash, you got cash?"

"Clever girl. Fuck me with your fingers, your tongue in my mouth - I've got cash in my bag."

Maddy pulled the bag up from the floor and flipped open one of the latches. "See?"

She peeled off three hundred-dollar notes and gave them to the girl. "Put the money in your panties, so it'll smell of your sex when we're done." She looked directly up at the girl. "If I had more time I'd fuck you, too."

"Next time," said the girl, spreading Maddy's lips wide and quickly taking her, two fingers forcibly in, then three.

"Ahh, yes, faster. Fuck. Good girl, that's..." Maddy bucked back, taken hard by the force of the girl's fingers thrusting into her cunt.

The girl leaned forward, her fingers fucking fast, her other hand pressing hard against one of Madelyn's tits, grinding her palm over the tight nipple.

"You like that, crazy lady? Nice little tits!"

She leaned further forward, taking Madelyn's mouth, fucking deep into it with her tongue. She twisted Madelyn's breast, sensing the woman wanted a sharp pain in a hurting place.

Maddy's own fingers were fast on her clit, finishing with a swirl what she'd begun earlier, bringing herself to a quick, high peak. Her cry as she came was stifled by the girl's mouth, her tongue thrusting deep. Maddy took the fuck into herself, throbbing with ecstasy.

When she was done, snapping herself into control, Maddy took the girl's cheeks in both her hands, holding her face before her. She looked deep into the girl's eyes, before kissing her again.

"You were good. Filthy, but good. Thank you." She sucked the girl's cunt wet fingers, her own wetness frothed and creamy white. She licked the girl's fingers clean.

The girl smiled. "I'm glad I could help. You're still a crazy bitch, though."

"You should be glad, for what I paid." But Maddy was smiling too. It was only money, but her orgasm grounded her, gave her back her certainty. She was thankful for that. "And yes, I am. Fucking crazy." She laughed, amused by the girl's astonishment, but glad she'd played along.

"Go on, tidy yourself up. Wash your hands. Make sure no-one comes in until I say. If anybody asks, I was feeling faint."

Maddy found her panties and slid them on, wiping herself first with toilet paper. She looked down at herself, and liked the pummelled redness of her sex. The girl hadn't been gentle. Maddy needed that.

She smoothed the dress down her legs, and put her shoes back on. She left the cubicle and went to a wash basin, where she cupped her hands under the tap and wet her face. The girl passed Maddy a towel; she too was respectable now, the money gone and a serious, concerned look on her face. Perfect," said Maddy, and kissed the girl. "You're very sweet."

"Thank you, Ma'am," the girl replied, bobbing in an exaggerated curtsey.

Maddy laughed, looking at herself in the mirror. "I should wipe all the lipstick off, don't you think. It's a mess."

"Probably, yes."

"What will they all be thinking, I wonder?" pondered Maddy, who didn't care at all.

"You felt faint, remember?"

"Ah yes, so very delicate. Thank you, my dear, for checking on me." Maddy smiled at the girl.

"All part of the service, milady." The girl grinned back, cheekily.

"Come on," said Maddy. "Look concerned as we walk out the door. Do I look half fucked?"

"Jesus, I don't know. What do you look like fully fucked?"

Maddy smiled. "Give me your number, and you might find out."

"Are you serious? You really are fucking crazy! Shit!"

Maddy left the rest-room, and made her way back to the dining room. Curious patrons looked up as she passed, she'd been gone so long. She looked straight ahead and ignored them.

She stopped walking and turned to the waitress. "Thank you," she said, "you were very kind. Your name. Would you tell me your name?"

"Juliette," the girl replied.

Maddy stared at Juliette for a long moment, then smiled, but the smile didn't reach her eyes.

"How very appropriate," she said softly.

"What do you mean?" the girl asked.

"You've not read de Sade? You should. Your namesake is one of his sluts."

"Fuck you," Juliette responded, her eyes flaring in anger.

"You just did, darling. Very well, too. I enjoyed it very much, your filthy fingers."

Their conversation was low, but this time her smile was real. Juliette was about to say something, but fell silent and turned away. Maddy went back to the table.

Adam looked up. "What was that all about?" he asked. "Are you all right? You've been gone fifteen minutes. I was beginning to worry."

"Adam, you're a darling. Thanks for sending the girl in. That *was* you?" She reached across the table to touch the back of his hand. "She was very sweet, looking after me. Her name's Juliette. Isn't that a pretty name?"

"Madelyn, this is the first time I've heard you talk like that. Are you sure you're okay?" He studied her. "I didn't think you talked 'pretty names'."

"It's not fair," Maddy pouted. "You get the girl to go all gushy, talking to the handsome man, but I don't get to do that?"

She teased him. "Ooo, Mister handsome man, can I suck your cock, please, pretty please?" She grinned. "Ooo, sir, it's so big. How will I get that down my throat?"

"Maddy, you're incorrigible. You know you can do that." He smiled, and she saw the heat in his eyes.

"Who? Me? Mister handsome man, you presume far too much!"

She laughed, enjoying the silly game she was playing, enjoying Adam's indulgence of her change in mood. She put her fingers up to his lips so he could smell the fresh soap and guess why she'd washed her hands.

He shook his head, and she saw the glint in his eyes, his wry smile. She thought he'd probably know.

"You're all right? You can still eat?" he asked.

"Oh yes, I'm famished. It's hard work, being me."

"Just as well I sent in some help, then."

She smiled a slow lazy smile, luxuriating in the knowledge that he knew.

"I asked the kitchen to wait," he said, signalling to Jean-Claude with a raised finger and a nod of his head.

"Normal services will be resumed, then?" Maddy asked, running two fingers down the back of his hand, the two fingers that had dipped into her sex and pulled the folds back from her clit. She looked at her fingers soft on his skin and remembered them hard in her flesh. Between her thighs, she felt the hot burn in her cunt, and wanted to see the girl close by, once again.

"Define normal, Maddy."

"Oh no, I'd better not. Then you'll only want better."

"Best, Madelyn, I always want best."

Ahh, she thought, so that's what he wants.

She leaned back, slowly trailing her fingers along his, down onto the tablecloth, down past the edge of the knife, her index finger moving towards herself in a single dragging slide on the cloth. She watched his eyes follow her finger tip as it came to the edge of the table, pointing down towards her centre. His eyes followed her finger until it slid off the cloth and dropped down. He raised his eyes to hers, where she was already waiting for his gaze. Still sitting back, Maddy held his gaze as she dropped her finger to the high slit in her dress and eased her legs apart, finding the edge of her panties.

She eased her slow finger down the slick of her lips, wincing as she felt the hot burn from Juliette's quick fuck. Her eyes lazily closed as she anointed her finger. She dragged her finger tip over her clit, shuddering in a last reminder. Opening her eyes to see Adam's eyes still on hers, she lifted her wet finger above the table and put it to his lips.

"Perfection, Mister Cain. Always strive for perfection."

She fucked her wet finger into his mouth just once, so he knew.

"Fuuck, Madelyn...."

She didn't need to respond; he was losing it. She smiled to herself, just creasing the edges of her eyes. He knew it too, and wanted it. Madelyn was working him out, but Adam would have to wait.

"Mademoiselle, the barramundi." Juliette placed the plate before Maddy and was rewarded with those genuine eyes, again.

"Sir, your *filet mignon*. Blue, as you ordered." She placed the plate before him, and was surprised he was distracted, didn't have time for her, not this time. She glanced back at Maddy, wondering what the hell was going on between these two.

Maddy saw the questioning look, and touched her fingers to the girl's wrist, as a reminder. Juliette looked down, feeling the touch, before slowly moving her hand away.

"Thank you, Juliette." She heard Adam's voice. "It is Juliette, isn't it?"

"Yes sir, Juliette."

She glanced down at Adam, and saw the distant look in his eyes fade as he focussed back on her. She smiled down at him as a gift, and his own smile in return was gentle, so very gentle. Juliette glanced back at Maddy and was perplexed, because her smile now was real, too. After the swift business in the toilet cubicle, she didn't expect that. Juliette had wondered what on earth made the woman tick; but three hundred bucks... she didn't care, that was more than her weekend's wages.

Juliette left them to their meal, and over the rest of the evening studied them discreetly, whenever she could, trying to establish their dynamic. She decided in the end they were like a pair of wild and beautiful cats, circling around each other on silent paws, wanting to fight but wouldn't. Juliette wondered what it would be like to be caught between them like delicate prey, and decided she'd try to find out.

When Madelyn asked for the bill, Juliette processed the credit card payment, and saw the fifty dollar tip. She placed the tip in the communal drawer, like they always did, to be shared amongst all of the staff. She then dipped inside her bra to retrieve the folded up notes, which she smoothed out and placed under the card in the bill-fold sleeve. She wrote her phone number on a piece of white paper and placed it under the card, on top of the money. Her heart beat fast, but she didn't know what else to do.

She placed the bill-fold by Maddy's hand, and quickly went back to the counter, as if nothing had happened. She couldn't look at the woman, so looked down at her hand instead, remembering the creamy froth of Maddy's cunt and the grip of it on her fingers.

"Adam, can you drive, please. I don't feel like driving down the hill. Straight back to your place, and I'll take the car from there."

Maddy closed her eyes all the way down the hill, trusting this man completely. Her hand on his leg felt the muscles tighten in his thigh each time he changed gear, the smooth up and down quite soothing. Once down the hill and in the city, she placed her hand on the back of his head, slowly stroking his hair. She sleepily opened her eyes and watched his concentration as he drove to his apartment.

"Will you come up?"

"Oh no, Mister Cain, I don't do that."

"I didn't think you would."

"Not on a first date, Adam. Remember what I said about being too fast?"

"Just as well I'm a patient man." He smiled at her, and she got a little closer, because he was waiting for the best.

Adam got out of the driver's seat, leaving the door open. He went around the back of the car, reaching down to open the passenger door. Maddy slid her long legs to the pavement, the fall of her dress revealing the creamy white flesh of her thigh and the bruised red slit of her sex. She reached up for his hand and he helped her out of the car.

She took his face in her hands, studying him intently for a long moment. She kissed him softly on the lips, holding the back of his neck as she did so, just a soft, gentle touch. She could love this man, if he let her.

"I'll call you, Adam. I promise."

He didn't need to say anything. Madelyn always delivered on her promises, in her own time, when she was ready.

Back at the restaurant Juliette was tidying the restroom and saw an envelope with her name written on it. Inside she found Madelyn's knickers, neatly folded, the three hundred dollars given back, and a note.

She read the note. "It's not payment, it's a promise. Buy yourself something beautiful and wear it next time. Madelyn."

Juliette stood, breathing the woman's animal smell deeply in. "You're still fucking crazy," she whispered.

She then realised Madelyn had her number, but she didn't have Madelyn's. She looked in the booking diary, but there was no number there, just Jean-Claude's immaculate writing.

8.00 pm. Table x 2. Madeline.

Jean-Claude had spelt her name wrong. It was Madelyn. Her partner had called her Maddy.

Dressing Juliette

"Juliette, hi, it's Maddy."

...

"Yes, from the restaurant last month."

...

"That's right. How could I forget?"

...

"You washed them? You're a darling... listen, did you buy something beautiful?"

...

"A gift, that's right. You didn't? Weren't sure what to get?"

...

"Okay, how about this..."

Maddy made arrangements to meet Juliette in town the following week. She then rang Adam to let him know he wasn't forgotten, and would he like to get together the weekend after this one?

"Oh no, Mister Cain. I don't do that. I'll come and pick you up, like before.

"No, no. I'll bring everything. Just yourself." She laughed at his reply. "Of course you will, you delicious man.

"Early afternoon. I'll confirm a time later. Bye."

"Juliette, there you are. I'm sorry I'm a little late." Madelyn wasn't sorry at all, as it was her way to set little tests where time was concerned, just to gauge reactions. She smiled as she remembered Adam's finger tapping on the dashboard clock in her car, *See, I'm right on time.*

Juliette looked up from the bench she was sitting on and put her phone away. "That's okay, I was just flicking through some catalogues -"

"To find something beautiful?" Maddy asked. "That's good, I want you to look beautiful. Wrapped up with a bow; what do you think?"

"You make me sound like a gift. Is that what I am? Someone's present?" Juliette stood up and faced Maddy. "What's going on, anyway? I gave you my number a month ago, and you've only just called."

"Oh, darling, you weren't waiting by the phone all that time, surely not?" Maddy laughed. "Silly girl. But that's very sweet."

"But I thought -"

"Do you know, that's exactly what Adam said. I said he should stop thinking."

"Who's Adam? Your partner at the restaurant? You're not a couple though, are you? You're not together."

Juliette was curious, remembering the attention she'd received from them both, wondering what it would be like to be tangled up between them. She remembered his admiring eyes and Madelyn's kiss, the raw passion of their sex. Juliette felt a weight in the base of her belly, picturing Madelyn's creaming froth on her fingers, seeing the woman before her now. *Next time.*

This was the next time. Juliette was more than curious, she was fascinated by this crazy woman who'd fucked with her mind in a toilet cubicle, then called her out of the blue. That night, after she'd got home, Juliette had relived the time with Maddy, and she'd come too. Not as fast as Maddy; she savoured the memory and took her time. She didn't quite believe that she'd done it, fucked Maddy fast with her fingers, but the envelope with its contents proved she'd been awake.

"Not a couple, no. How could you tell?" Maddy asked.

"Well, you arranged it all. You made the booking, picked up the bill. Your car, that's not really a man's car, is it? A little sports car like that. I saw you arrive. You were driving."

Juliette went on, pointing out something else: "And you in the bathroom, that was all about you, wasn't it? Seems to me, that night was your night. Like you'd arranged a date or something."

She stopped talking for a moment, thinking, then asked Maddy, "Is that what this is, some kind of a date? You and me?"

"Do you know, darling, I think it might be," Maddy replied.

"Well, where are we going then, you and I? To eat a peach?"

"To eat a peach?" Maddy didn't get the reference.

"Let us go then, you and I,
When the evening is spread out against the sky
Like a patient etherised upon a table..."

Juliette narrated the lines of the poem, and as she did so, they started walking. "And later, the narrator says, 'Shall I part my hair behind? Do I dare eat a peach?', and there's a line about flannel trousers and walking on a beach, but I can't remember exactly how they go."

She looked up at Madelyn walking beside her. "It's a T.S.Eliot poem, 'The Love Song of J. Alfred Prufrock.'"

"'Etherised on a table.' I like that," said Maddy.

Juliette looked at her, and wondered if the woman was all there.

"Where do you get this from?" Maddy went on. "Your poetry?"

"English Lit degree," Juliette replied. "It's why I work as a waitress."

"Really? English Lit? You'll get on with Adam, then. That's what he's got. English Literature and Double History. Quite what it's got to do with his work, I don't know; but there you are."

Juliette digested this new information and they walked on, turning a corner into an alley with a range of boutique shops on both sides. "Is that why you want me to be beautiful, to be a gift for Adam?" she asked.

Madelyn stopped, and Juliette walked on another two steps alone, before she too stopped and turned to face Maddy. She couldn't interpret the look on the other woman's face.

"Actually, no." Maddy replied. "I like my own beautiful things. Adam might be one of them eventually, but I'm still figuring that out, how to do that. He's wilful, and I'm running out of 'no's' for an answer." She laughed, as much at herself and her self-made dilemma, as at her continued saying no to Adam. *Oh no, Mister Cain, I don't do that.*

Juliette crossed her fingers to remember a point. Maddy was showering her with concepts and revelations, and she had to take them one at a time or completely lose her way. By a tacit agreement, they stood still in the street, Maddy having ushered Juliette out of the flow of pedestrians with a guiding touch on her arm. Perhaps Maddy needed clarity in a still place too, from time to time.

"So," pondered Juliette, "I'm a beautiful thing, but I'm to be your beautiful thing, is that it? Not for him?"

"I guess," Maddy replied, "since I'm paying; yes, that makes you mine, doesn't it?"

"I guess it does. But you're not paying. I'm volunteering." Juliette said it, stepping into the panther's den, her head held high and her throat exposed.

Madelyn looked at her, astonished at what she'd just heard.

"And at the moment, you're trying to snare Adam by not letting him pay for anything, either, but you're paying him attention, is that it? You're making yourself the prize, but it's early days. So he's dangling?"

"Clever girl. Yes, I suppose that's it." *What Madelyn wants, Madelyn gets.* "He's no puppet though, he won't always do what I want." She paused. "He's rather delightful, really. Quite a challenge."

Juliette digested all this, and Maddy watched her do it, fascinated by the speed of the girl's thought process, realising that she might not be so totally alone, after all.

"So," Juliette concluded, uncrossing her fingers, "why don't we, you and I, eat a peach with Adam and have twice as much fun?"

"My sweet god, you're ruthless. 'Etherise him on a table,' is that it?" Madelyn looked at the girl with a sudden new appreciation.

"Something like that," Juliette said, and started walking.

"Fuuck," said Maddy in admiration. "You're quick off the mark."

"I beat you up a hundred bucks, remember. And we'd only just met."

"You did. Nobody's done that before. I'm impressed." Madelyn walked along beside the girl.

"Let's go buy me beautiful things," said Juliette, "if I'm going to be your prize."

They turned into a narrow doorway and made their way up a flight of stairs. Juliette stepped ahead, with Madelyn admiring the sway of her ass under a long flowing skirt. The girl wore a pair of Doc Martens, surprisingly small and somehow quite delicate. One of the stairs creaked as she stepped on it, startling Maddy from her delight.

At the top of the stairs there was a small landing, with several closed doors leading off it. Maddy pushed open one of the doors, and a discreet buzzer sounded at the back of the shop.

"I buy all my frillies here," said Madelyn, as they entered the shop. "It's like a little Paris."

Juliette, who could only afford Target, stopped inside the entrance and was spellbound. The shop was crowded with racks of clothing down one side, shelves of lingerie, soaps and scents down the other; and near the back, a floor length mirror reflected a wide display space. Juliette saw a pretty girl in the mirror, and recognised herself standing there. She reached out to caress a skein of soft fabric beside her.

"My god," she whispered, "I didn't know this place was here. It's beautiful, so luxurious." She breathed in the scents of the shop, looking around, up and down. "It's wonderful."

"Oh yes," replied Maddy, "it's quite divine."

"Madelyn, my darling, my beauty, who DO we have here? Let me see her!"

A flamboyantly camp man in his late sixties or early seventies emerged from the back of the shop with his hands outstretched in greeting, a beaming smile on his face. Immaculately dressed in pin-striped trousers and a silver brocade waistcoat, with pomaded hair, he air-kissed Madelyn on both cheeks before turning to Juliette. Taking both her hands in his, he stepped back to see her properly.

"Oh my goodness, Madelyn, where DID you find her? Isn't she delicious?" He swirled around Juliette, before dropping to his knee and, taking her hand in his, kissing the backs of her fingers.

"Bonnard," he announced himself, "at your service, Mademoiselle."

"Juliette," she replied, laughing, too astonished to think straight, but with a wide smile on her face from his outrageous performance.

"Juliette? Oh my dear, HOW delectable, how it CLICKS off the tongue: JuliETTE!"

"Bonnard, you old cliché, stop it at once before you make yourself sick." Madelyn's voice was full of affection for the man. "We need your demonic arts to make Juliette even more beautiful than she is."

He looked at Juliette with a practised eye. "Of course. My demonic arts. My dear, where SHALL we start?"

Juliette knew she didn't need to answer. She watched as Bonnard went to the front door and locked it with an ancient, elaborate key.

"There," he said, "we won't be interrupted. I'm quite exclusive, it's part of my charm."

"Bonnard, it's part of your act," said Madelyn. "Don't dally. I want to see Juliette at her best. Chop chop!"

"Miss Madelyn, a master at his craft needs time, as well you know. One mustn't rush." He glared at Maddy, only to be ignored.

"Ttt Ttt," he clicked his tongue. "Have it your own way. I've made you tea, it's by the chair."

He fluttered his hand to the back of the shop where there was a large comfortable chair opposite the long mirror, pushed far back against the wall. Any occupant of the chair would have a clear view of the mirror and its reflection, but be veiled in shadow themselves.

He turned to Juliette, taking her by the hand. "Come, my dear, let's sort out your sizes. Let's see you first, then we'll cover you up."

He led her down to the end of the shop and placed her before the mirror. Behind her, and she was already in shadows, Madelyn was seated in the chair, leaning back comfortably with one leg drawn up, watching the display before her. Bonnard, ever the maestro, knew what she wanted, and would wrap her gift up perfectly, tied with a bow.

But first, "Let's see what you look like, my darling. May I?"

Bonnard didn't say what he wanted to do, but Juliette stood willingly, her arms by her sides.

"Of course you may. Whatever you need to do."

She took a deep, shuddering breath, and fell within herself, into her own sensation. Nothing else existed, and she could have heard a pin drop. She placed herself in Bonnard's hands, knowing that Maddy was watching.

Once he got down to business, Bonnard lost the affectation and his *outré* campiness. His voice became a steady murmur as he started up a running commentary, but only for himself and Juliette. Maddy sat watching, not needing commentary at all, just watching. She soaked the girl up with her gaze, getting wet.

"First, these boots. Quite fine and divine for the day, let's keep them, shall we? But for openings and galleries, our evening places, high heels, don't you think? But look, such little feet, how astonishing, where did they come from? Foot up, darling, while we take these boots off; aaand the other one, good girl. A four inch heel, no more. Three might be better, such little feet.

"Oh, you sensible thing, cotton socks so your feet don't rub in those boots. Lift up, there's a darling, and let's curl them off, shall we, one by one. Hmmm. Ohh, that's very nice. How divine!"

Juliette wasn't surprised when Bonnard bought the socks to his nose, inhaling her scent like a cork. She suspected he was a connoisseur of many things, clearly delighting in her body. She imagined his hands on a perfume bottle, reading the label first, turning it over to read the back.

"Oh look, tiny tidy toes and an acceptable colour already. We'll fix you up with a pedicure next door, Katy's wonderfully quick."

He got to his feet, and took the hem of Juliette's top in his hands. "Hands up, darling, over your head. I'm not going to shoot you, not at all. Up we go."

In one smooth movement he lifted the garment up over her head and up her arms, revealing Juliette's naked torso, her high breasts, and two dark shadows of hair *au naturel* in her armpits.

"Oh my, look at you, a natural girl. How perfect."

"Smell me, if you like," said Juliette, her voice so low only Bonnard could hear.

"Thank you, my darling, but later. I mustn't get distracted. Now, your brassiere, what size?"

"I'm a thirty-two - "

"Oh darling, I was talking to myself, it's a silly habit, I know. No need to tell me, I can see you perfectly well. Sizes on labels, pah! It's all by eye, always by eye. Miss Maddy over there, even she doesn't know her own sizes, a tall girl like her? I remember them for her. A label would seem quite offensive, don't you think?"

Juliette was beginning to understand this man, his vintner to her grape, a connoisseur of a little bit of everything. She brought her arms down and rested her hands on his upper arms, her breasts settling to their standing shape, for his eyes. Her nipples were tight, lifting two pierced bars away from the curve of her breasts.

"Ah, what's this I see? A little decoration on your pretty breasts, how lovely, very lovely. Did it hurt much, when they were pierced?"

Juliette nodded. "It did, yes. It hurt."

"Did you like the hurt, a joyous little pain?"

Juliette nodded again, remembering the sharp stab and the long dull ache as her flesh healed. "I did like it, yes. In a stabbing and aching kind of way." Her nipples, now, were thick and firm.

"It's not new for you, then? Do you play?"

Bonnard looked Juliette straight in the eye for a long moment, and she nodded a third time.

"Sometimes. When I can."

He smiled. "You've found a good one here, Maddy. You'll see." He raised his voice so Maddy could hear.

Juliette looked at Madelyn in the mirror, and saw she had one hand inside her blouse, caressing a breast. Her eyes looked hooded and sleepy, and Juliette knew she'd been gazing at her back, looking at her. Juliette's sex bloomed at the thought of that gaze, and she wondered how wet the other woman was, just from looking and wanting to possess her.

"But Miss Juliette, now we must see the rest of you, if we're to cover you all up. May I?"

There was no doubt in Juliette's head, none at all. She took her hands away from Bonnard's arms, and spread them wide. He carefully undid the buttons on the waist-band of her skirt, and unzipped the zip at the side. The cloth fell away from Juliette's hips, leaving her standing naked before him.

"Ahh, turn around, let me see," said Madelyn, leaning forward to look.

Juliette turned to face Madelyn, gazing at her. She saw Maddy's eyes move up and down her legs and body, pausing at her heart-shaped bush, the little curve of her belly, her tight nippled breasts; then Juliette deliberately turned away. Her bottom was lovely, too.

"Isn't she wonderful?" said Bonnard, playing his hands over Juliette's curves, hovering two inches from her body. "So very delicious, I could eat her all up!"

He'd not touched her skin once, other than holding her hands, but she felt caressed all over. If this was what being wrapped up as a gift meant, she'd take a hundred ribbons and bows.

"Wait," said Madelyn. "Come here. I want to see you, up close. My eyes are too far away."

Juliette looked to Bonnard as if for permission, it was his shop after all. But she supposed if Madelyn was the customer, he would let her out of his hands for five minutes. Or ten, whatever it took, depending on Maddy's caprices.

Bonnard seemed eager. "Oh yes, my darling, let her see."

He clapped his hands together, as if he was about to get a reward. Perhaps he was. Juliette raised a hand and spread her fingers wide. Bonnard laced his fingers through hers, giving her hand a quick squeeze, then let it go. She was in his care, after all.

Confidently, for Juliette if nothing else was confident, she stepped the four steps it took to stand in front of Madelyn. She stood quite still, her hands by her sides, waiting for instructions. Her senses were heightened, her eyes bright, and she looked straight ahead at a spot on the back wall. All movement was peripheral now, the stillness all in herself.

She heard Madelyn sigh, "Oh yes," and Juliette smiled. She really was very beautiful, Madelyn couldn't not want her.

Madelyn did want her.

"Closer, darling."

Her voice was low, whiskey soothed with honey, and the slightly cracked edge on it made Juliette's heart thrill, that she could affect a heartless woman so. She knew now that Maddy was cold inside, making her wait, making Adam wait; and she stood with her head held high, knowing this woman wanted her. She took a small step forward, deliberately not close enough.

"Look, Bonnard, she makes me come to her."

Behind her, Juliette heard Bonnard chuckle. "She's got a mind of her own, this one does."

"God," said Maddy, "what's wrong with me? I seem to be surrounding myself with them at the moment. Minds of their own."

"It's because you weren't looking," Juliette said. "But we're here anyway, despite you, not because of you."

"Ouch! So young, yet so wise."

"Does she remind you of anyone, Madelyn?" Bonnard asked.

Maddy laughed softly. "She certainly does. Yes, she most certainly does."

She leaned forward and gently tapped Juliette's ankle. The girl moved one foot away from the other. Maddy tapped the other ankle, and Juliette moved that one too. Her feet were a foot and a half apart, opening up the top of her thighs for Maddy's closer inspection.

Kneeling at Juliette's feet, Maddy ran both hands slowly up the outside of her calves and thighs, learning the tightness of the girl's muscle and the softness of her skin. She ran her hands over the curved wideness of Juliette's hips and into her narrow waist, then up her torso. Juliette stood waiting, absorbing the sensation, the slow and curious embrace.

"Arms up," said Maddy, and Juliette raised her arms, exposing again the soft trails of hair in the hollows. Madelyn ran both palms over the light brown hair, enjoying the faint tickle and the heat. "Quite lovely," she said, "so soft."

She ran her hands back down Juliette's body, sliding them around to cup her breasts, feeling their weight, the tight nipples and the bars hard in her palms. She experimentally tugged the two bars, and was pleased to see Juliette shift her feet, to better balance herself as she ever so slightly swayed. Maddy saw the quick intake of breath into the girl's belly, such a sweet little curve and a crease.

Maddy's own nipples were long and and thick, pulling up the peaks of her small breasts into hard cones. Her breasts ached with lust, heating fast, and the tightness behind them spread through her body. She took in a deep breath and calmed herself. Holding one of Juliette's breasts, she cupped the younger girl's sex in the palm of her hand, pressing up to feel her heat.

Juliette sighed, and placed her hands on Maddy's head, pulling her closer to her body. "Hold my pussy, that's nice. You can have me, if you like."

"In the chair," Madelyn said, and didn't quite believe how softly she'd said it. "Lie down so you're comfortable." Usually she didn't care.

Still holding her hands to Maddy's head, Juliette guided the other woman to her feet, and Maddy let herself be guided. Juliette turned and sat in the chair, leaned back and spread wide her legs, exposing her sex. She looked up at Maddy and smiled. It was a reversal of the moment when she'd opened the door to Maddy's cubicle, not knowing what she'd see. Now she was the one opening herself wide to be fucked, but she was still the wanted one, which pleased her.

Across the display space, Bonnard sat back in his own chair in his own still world, just watching. He wasn't done with dressing Juliette, so his reward was yet to come. Meanwhile, Maddy was unexpectedly generous, and had angled herself on the floor so that Bonnard could easily see the girl's sweet cunt and the tidy heart of hair on her mound. He remembered the touch of the girl's fingers through his, and liked her more because of it.

"Fuck me with your mouth, slowly," Juliette instructed, sensing that Maddy, momentarily, was no longer in charge. Juliette's willingness pulled the control from her mistress.

Across the carpet Juliette saw Bonnard nod, as if to affirm her choice. *So, Madelyn likes to be told, sometimes.* Juliette tucked the knowledge away, and lay back, taking Madelyn's head in her hands, again.

"Not fast like you wanted that night, fucked fast in a toilet by a stranger, slut fucking slut, all cash and cold comfort." Juliette remembered Bonnard's gentle commentary, how it lulled her; and she reversed it now for Madelyn, provoking her with her crude sex before giving Maddy the comfort of her own sweet cunt, all swollen and warm and given, given to Maddy, wide and wet.

"You don't need fury with me, Maddy, my three fingers fucking quick till you hurt, your breath panting as you kicked down the door, your long legs fucked wide open, your own fingers digging in, before I came in and made you come..."

And as she spoke, like an actress on a stage with Yorick's skull in her hand, Juliette held Maddy's head firm in her hands six inches away from her cunt, so the other woman could smell her, could see her glistening lips, could see a heartbeat in the hollow of her thigh if she looked; so that Maddy could see what she wanted in front of her, before...

Before Juliette swung a leg quickly over Madelyn's head, and rolled her body away, presenting the voluptuous curves of her ass instead.

She heard a swift intake of breath and Bonnard's astonished, "Oh my!" Juliette knew the cleft of her sex would be just as plump, just as succulent and inviting, curved between the backs of her thighs. She knew too, clever girl, that her invitation to be slow would make Maddy want the opposite, and Juliette really wanted that. Her fast words were her own reminder, and she'd already pleasured herself slowly, at night. Juliette knew the power of words, being an actress as well as a waitress.

She heard Maddy hiss with pleasure, "Yesss..."

To reinforce her offering, Juliette moved again in the chair, kneeling with her knees against its arms, her head up against the back of it, her arms braced wide around the back of it too, ready to be taken like a bitch in heat. Her breasts were crushed up against the back of the chair, and she ached, she ached, she ached...

to be fucked; and Maddy took her cunt into her mouth, gripping the cheeks of her bottom and spreading them wide, opening up access to her back hole and the succulent flesh of her sex. Madelyn gave one long flat tongued lick from Juliette's clit right up to her ass crack, her spit and saliva all wet, before sucking her mouth to Juliette's cunt, heating her there, sucking hard on her sex.

Juliette moaned, and thrust back her body, driving her sex wide wet onto Maddy's face, her mouth. "Quick, fuck slut, make me come!"

Maddy thrust into her with her tongue deep and hard, fucking Juliette fast. She reached up the girl's body and took her hanging breasts in both hands. She pulled them down, pressed them up, felt their weight, felt her own nipples rock tight. After fifteen, twenty tongue fucking seconds, Maddy found the angles all wrong, but she had the taste of the girl in her mouth. So she moved up Juliette's body, finding the girl's mouth, giving her own taste back with her tongue and her lips.

At the same time she found Juliette's cunt with her own long fingers, and gave the girl three fingers, deep and fast, fucking into her body hard like the girl had finger fucked her. Juliette bucked and moaned into the thrusts.

"Fuck, it's easier," Juliette exclaimed, and twisted her body so she was once again sprawled on her back in the chair, with Maddy's long fingers deep in her slick, aching cunt, and it was the toilet cubicle all over again, their mouths hot and furious, mashing their lips together.

"Fuck me, bitch, fucking next time, you made me wait, fuck you..." Juliette goaded Maddy, and it worked, her mouth even hungrier, the palm of her hand grinding down onto Juliette's mound to hurt her, pressing in circles around her clit. Maddy fucked the girl, taking one furred arm pit into her mouth and sucking in that scent like another cunt, returning to

Juliette's mouth and giving her back the pheromone taste, her tongue and lips scented with the girl's body.

"Oh my," uttered Bonnard, "such delight!" and Juliette promised herself to give him that too, when he finally dressed her, give him her body's taste, sweet delight. Her wet cunt, the scent from it, when Bonnard dressed her. She pictured him breathing her in.

She was getting closer, and Maddy sensed it. She began to slow down her fuck.

"Bitch. No you fucking don't, not me, not Juliette!"

By naming herself, she became disembodied, but she wasn't about to let Maddy deny her.

"I made you come, quick and fast. Don't be fucking selfish. My turn now, or you don't get what you want, next time."

Juliette took the risk of denying next time, but she also took Madelyn's head in her hands, and forced the other woman down to her succulent juice, the pleasure of her cunt, and it worked.

Madelyn decided, *I wanted to fuck this girl,* so she did. She forgot about herself in that moment, and found herself responding to Juliette's desire, her rhythm. She swirled her tongue slow and steady, then faster and faster, holding the girl deeper in her mouth, but slower, much slower, ooohh, and quicker, and fast.

She took Juliette up and up, into her pleasure; and as she did so Maddy felt a deep throb in the base of her own belly, and it connected to the aching depths behind her breasts and warmed her with a delicious fullness, her tits so tight. She wanted a fuck, but could wait. Her breasts ached. She wanted this girl, this Juliette, this girl who was so like her. Madelyn wanted to come, but she'd wait.

Maddy took Juliette up into that beautiful place where she came, all opened up and taken, shuddering sweet. Juliette came, and Maddy held her sex in her mouth as she did so, gently holding her heat, all still. Juliette shuddered again, pleasure trembling through her. She found one of Maddy's hands and laced her fingers through the other woman's, and they became still.

Juliette stroked Maddy's hair, and slowly relaxed her legs, her muscles tight from thrusting her sex up to Maddy's fingers. "I'm smiling," she whispered, and she was. The air in the shop was still. Her perfume mingled with the other scents there.

"Bonnard, darling, could you make some more tea? And a cup for Juliette?"

Madelyn leaned down to kiss the girl on the lips, mixing all her tastes together. She helped Juliette to her feet, wrapping her shoulders in a shawl. "Keep warm, until Bonnard is ready, you mustn't get cold." Maddy surprised herself, caring so much.

"I'm not cold," said Juliette, who shivered again, hearing Madelyn's emotion cracked voice. She had the crazy woman's feelings running strong, and thought that might be unusual. She smiled a little smile.

Bonnard must have seen the smile. "Oh look, the cat's got the cream, lucky cat."

"Oh please, Bonnard, she's a kitten, not a cat." Madelyn, once again imperious and in control, took her place in the chair and took the proffered cup. "Finish the devil's work and dress the girl, there's a dear. A summer walk in a garden, keep that in mind."

"A promenade, Miss Juliette? A long flowing dress, something Edwardian, something with lace? We'll see. But first, we must measure you up. Here, darling, stand here. That's my girl, shoulders back, nice and tall. Oh my goodness, look at those breasts, look how full they are now. Hmm, let me see..."

Bonnard studied Juliette for perhaps ten seconds, his eyes up and down, measuring her perfectly.

"Tilt," he said, touching her chin. Juliette looked up, and Bonnard judged her throat too.

"Perfect. Shawl around you darling, stay warm. I'll just be a moment. Colours, let me think... she's got quite the dusky skin, a little gypsy perhaps..."

Bonnard was speaking to himself, steepling his fingers together in thought as he moved down the aisle of the shop to gather up some lingerie.

Juliette took the opportunity to focus on her still places, the heat from her orgasm still warm, the softness of Madelyn's hand in hers, their lingering breath still slow.

The hard fuck of Maddy's fingers might give her a bruise, but it would be no different to Maddy's raw cunt in the cubicle. She wondered if their relationship would ever be gentle during sex, or only afterwards. She wondered too, at herself. What was she really doing here?

"Dreaming, darling?" Bonnard brought her back to earth.

Juliette opened her eyes, placing a hand on Bonnard's shoulder to regain her balance. She parted her legs just a little, and saw him breathe her scent in. She gently squeezed his shoulder. "Don't forget to smell me," she whispered.

"Oh darling, I won't forget. Thank you." He looked at her for a moment, and Juliette saw a myriad of emotions flicker in his eyes. Clarity suddenly struck her, some quick insight into this extraordinary man, this man who clearly adored women.

"Bonnard, before you came here, were you always a dresser, a woman's tailor? Or did you learn something else?"

"Ahh, clever girl. You've found me. Yes, I trained as a *parfumier* in London, but drove myself mad and had to stop."

"Mad, Bonnard? Why?"

"Why, my angel, why? She asks me why I went mad, Madelyn; what lies should I tell her?"

There was a long pause before Madelyn replied. "The truth, my friend, so she understands why I brought her here."

"The truth? Oh sweet girl, this old heart and the truth? I'm not sure we get along, but I'll try. It won't take long.

"The art of a perfumer, my darling, is to find the essence of a scent, to find the right chemicals from many places, many natural things, and swirl them all together," his finger swirled like a teaspoon's whirlwind in a cup, "into a perfect flavour, a wonderful scent."

He traced a finger down the soft skin of Juliette's cheek, and she tilted her head to acknowledge it. "Then we find a delicate pulse, a little heart beat; because that's where the heat comes from, my darling, the heat that makes it all ignite." His fingers splayed into two wide fans, "A wonderful floral fragrance like a rose, or a darker taste like aniseed or liquorice. Delicious, is it not? We all know how it works." His eyes were bright, and glistened.

Juliette listened, enthralled; and between his words, pins dropped and whispers were silent, and nothing existed at all. "Go on," she said, knowing where this would end, but wanting Bonnard's melodious voice to tell her.

"And me, silly me, *le grand Bonnard*, I thought I could capture the most magnificent scent of all, a woman after her pleasure." He looked at Juliette with such depth in his eyes that she'd fall, if she didn't hold on to his arms. "Of course, I was foolish. How could I even start to do that, capture women in a bottle?

"But me, pay no heed, it was silly. But that's how it all started; my darling, lovely girls and generous ladies would leave little bits of themselves behind, their cotton gussets, their slips of lace, and their naughty tainted knickers. They indulged me, and the idea of it! Ahh, they wanted themselves caught up in a bottle, too. What fun, to be remembered like that, on a wrist!

"I had quite a collection, until I burnt them all." His fingers exploded the air into a flaming ball. "Such an impossible thing. You are all... so different, you see, all so utterly unique.

"And of course, I had to give them all replacements, my dear. Little froths of cloth, satin whispers against their skin, velvet softness on their breasts, soft cottons on their nether lips. I became quite a cloth collector, my darling, and a devil with a sewing machine! And soon enough, more London ladies came visiting, and bringing their daughters too, and your Bonnard was quite engulfed. Word of mouth, quite a chatter, and Monsieur Bonnard so very discreet, and such fabulous hands! And listen to him talk, oh how you'll smile!

"So you see, my darling, it's really just a circus; but instead of a merry-go-round that just makes you dizzy, it's your knickers up and down like your grandmother's, and such a wonderful fuss."

Juliette laughed, beginning to understand this adorable man. "Will you sniff me all up, and put me in your latest collection? I think I'd like that."

"He already has." Maddy laughed too, a joyous chuckle. "It's the only payment he really wants, to be so close to your luscious limbs that your aroma envelopes him while he dresses you up and makes you worth undressing. I have to insist he takes money. He only does it so he can feed the cat."

"Oh Madelyn, that's not true," Bonnard protested. He winked at Juliette and whispered, "I don't even have a cat."

For the next half an hour Bonnard fitted Juliette with three perfect bras, matching knickers, stockings and a garter belt. "Ttt Ttt, that colour's all wrong, let's try another... oh, my darling, that's perfect! Look at you." Juliette did, and adored herself in Bonnard's mirror.

"We'll find a pretty dress next door," said Madelyn. "Here, we stay close to the skin."

She stood up, and came across to the dressing space, where Juliette stood in her new lingerie, dark shades of satin and silk set off against her glowing skin. "Did you find the perfect one, Bonnard?" she asked.

"I did, Madelyn. You'll find it fits just right. In the box, here you are." Bonnard handed Maddy a small box, velvet covered with a small golden clasp. At first, Juliette thought it might be jewellery, but it was so much better than that.

Madelyn took a black lace choker with a simple criss-cross pattern out of the box and placed it carefully around Juliette's throat. She kissed Juliette once on the lips and placed her finger there, a silence, nothing said.

Bonnard was right, it fitted perfectly. He'd judged her throat, just right.

"Thank you, Bonnard, you wonderful man," and Maddy kissed him, too.

"My pleasure, Madelyn, as always."

As they left the shop, wearing her boots and her flowing dress once again, and wearing her lingerie too, Juliette flung her arms around Bonnard's neck and kissed him, a third loving kiss.

She didn't say a word, she didn't need to. He'd paid her enough already, by breathing her deeply in.

The Garden

"Umm, hi, is that Adam?"

...

"Yes, Adam Cain, that's who I'm after. You're that Adam? Good."

...

"It's Juliette. You might remember me, from the restaurant last month? With Madelyn... yes, Maddy. That's right".

...

"Anyway, Maddy asked me to call you, to say we'll be there in fifteen minutes. But to be downstairs, we'll be in a different car. Hers is too small."

...

"Going to? I don't know, she's not said."

...

"Yes, this is my phone... no, I don't have it. She calls me, but it's always a blocked call."

...

Juliette laughed. "I guess so. But at least you've got my number now, and I've got yours."

...

"She might not like that..." She laughed again. "Fifteen minutes, then. I'm looking forward to it. Bye, yes, see you."

Juliette ended the call, and turned to Maddy, seated beside her in the rear seat of the car. "He said, since neither of us have your number, we should call each other. I think I'd like that. He sounds very nice. Where's he from again? That accent..."

"Juliette, darling, you're chattering. Nerves or excitement?"

"Both," replied Juliette. "I don't know what to expect."

"Neither do I, darling. But Adam's just so... quiet."

"Still waters run deep?" Juliette wondered.

"I hope so." Maddy registered where she was. "Turn left at the next lights, then the second right."

"Okay," said their driver.

"That's why I like him," mused Maddy. "He's so calm, so still. It drives me crazy, but I can't avoid his charm."

"Do you want to?" asked Juliette. "Avoid his charm, I mean."

"Oh no, I couldn't do that," Madelyn replied, and they both laughed. Madelyn took Juliette's hand in hers, between them on the seat. The grey leather was cold.

Adam was waiting on the pavement outside his apartment block when the car pulled up. Summonsed by Madelyn's wave from the rear window on the passenger side, he came towards the car. After a moment his face lit up with a broad grin, some recognition or other, some amusement.

"Get in the front," said Madelyn.

"With pleasure," he replied, still amused. "With my old mate, James." He opened the passenger door, looked in, grinned, and sat down. "Maate, long time, no see! How are you? Still driving the old Beemer, I see. New tyres, yet?"

"You know each other, then?" asked Madelyn. "What a coincidence. He was just the first Uber driver who came along with the right sized car."

"Oh yes, my old friend, James. He was rather... judgemental, shall we say, on a short ride a little while ago. The looks he can give, Maddy, glancing in the rear-view mirror. Goodness me, how he judged two innocent men."

The driver glared at him, clearly remembering the smug shit beside him, and the long-haired youth with the awkward bag.

"But he'll be confused now, me with two women."

Adam acknowledged Juliette, turning in the seat to greet her. "Hello, Juliette. Lovely to see you again. I love the dress, very summery."

"Leave him be, Adam. Remember what you said to me, at the restaurant." Madelyn grew tired quickly when it wasn't her toying.

Besides, Adam needed to be told and unsettled, and what better place to start, than right here at the beginning.

"Yes, sorry Madelyn, you're right. Too easy. Sorry, mate, do as she says. I would."

"You will, Adam, when I'm ready." Madelyn said, no emotion given away in her voice.

"Mate, you're in trouble," the driver whispered, feeling redeemed.

"Your opinion, driver, is not required." Maddy observed. "Just drive. You do know where we're going?"

"Yes ma'am, ten minutes."

"Ma'amselle, please. You see, Adam, it's quite easy to be nice, when you want to be."

"I'll pay attention, Madelyn, next time."

"Oh, you will, Mister Cain, you will. I have no doubt about that, none at all."

The driver smirked, *you're fucked, mate,* and Juliette smiled quietly to herself. She squeezed Maddy's hand, and was rewarded by a brief pressure back. Adam swallowed, and looked straight ahead.

Madelyn sat back, the wind through the open rear window warm against her skin, blowing strands of hair about her face. She reached forward with her left hand, gently placing the tips of her thumb and forefinger against Adam's neck, as if measuring him. She smiled. It would fit nicely, she thought. Madelyn wanted him now, and would have him. What Adam wanted no longer mattered, he just didn't know that yet.

The car pulled up beside a short, gravelled walk to a gate, surrounded by landscaped bushes and trees, a vibrant spread of colour. The driver got out and flipped the boot release with his remote. He reached in to extract a picnic basket and some rugs, which he set down a short way along the path. He then opened the rear door for Juliette, admiring her legs as she stepped out of the car. At the same time, Adam got out and opened Madelyn's door, reaching in for her hand.

She flowed gracefully from the vehicle, a long skirt splitting around a longer leg; no stockings, bare skin. Adam's eyes narrowed in appreciation at the tight vest top she was wearing, clinging to her small and braless breasts.

Madelyn smiled, liking that he liked what he saw, and wondered how far she could push him. Clearly, he wanted her. Could she make him want her, make him beg, tumble him right over his edge? She wanted something more than desire, she wanted something uncontrollable, out of control. The thought vaguely crossed her mind that she might need that too, in herself, as well as want it. Perhaps they might fall off their cliffs together, she wryly thought, each too proud to save the other. She looked at Adam with a new appreciation - nobody had triggered *that* thought before. Damn the man, finding a weakness in Maddy?

"Something amusing you, Madelyn?" he asked.

"Actually, yes," she replied cryptically, but gave him no enlightenment. Was this why she liked the man so much, because she wanted him quite badly? She just wasn't sure what for. What was that poem of Juliette's again, something laid out on a table?

She recovered herself. "Adam. I'm so glad you could make it. It's a perfect day for a picnic, don't you think?" She pecked him on the cheek, stroking her hand down his jaw, directing his gaze to hers. "I invited Juliette. She's a sweet thing, I hope you don't mind. You can talk poetry while I watch."

"Watch what, Madelyn?"

"You'll see. Did you wear your watch? Oh good, you did. Good boy." Maddy reached out her hand. "May I have it, please?"

Adam raised his eyebrow, curious, but undid the metal band, and passed his watch to her.

She slipped it on her own, more slender, wrist and admired it, turning her hand back and forth. "There. Your time is my time, now. Let me go check with your man, to collect us."

She went across to the driver and made a show of pointing at the watch, sorting out times.

Adam turned to Juliette. "Well, that was strange. What's she got of yours?"

Juliette turned to him, touching her fingers to the delicate choker at her throat. "Me. All of me. And she's bought me beautiful clothes. She said something about women being dressed to impress women, undressed to impress men, so perhaps we're going to find that out."

"She does like an orchestration, Maddy, doesn't she?"

"She likes more than that," replied Juliette, remembering her fingers fucking Maddy, and Maddy's mouth on hers. She was curious to see what Maddy had planned for Adam and her.

She appraised the man before her, thinking she would know him very well by the time Maddy was done. Juliette didn't mind the idea of that, thinking back to the restaurant where she'd imagined baring her neck to both his and Maddy's teeth. She was willing, but she vaguely thought Adam might fight. Now *that* might be exciting to watch. Juliette felt a little shiver on her skin, even though the air was still and warm.

She looked up at Adam's grey-blue eyes and saw everything more sharply. His gaze, looking back at her, was like a calmness in a still place. Maybe that's what Maddy wanted, to crack that calm, to see him undone. Or, to fall into that still, deep pool herself, and find herself undone. One could never tell with Maddy.

Juliette wondered what Maddy did with people when she got bored, and she also remembered the negotiation outside the toilet door, when she'd worked the woman up from two hundred to three hundred bucks, and how Maddy hadn't expected that. She had something of the crazy woman's measure, but wasn't exactly sure what.

She knew something of herself, too, but was curious about Adam. Where did he fit in to all of this? Who was he? She linked her arm through his, but wasn't sure if she was laying a claim or becoming a companion. Adam looked down at her, but she didn't have time to read his reaction.

"Good, that's settled," said Maddy, coming up to them. "The car's all sorted, to collect us. I just need to call him. Adam, darling, can you carry the hamper? Juliette and I will bring the rugs." She bent down to pick up a rug, and started walking down the path. "I wonder if there's anybody else here, at this time of day?"

"What if there is?" asked Juliette. "What will it matter?"

"Oh, you know I like my privacy, darling."

"But it's a public garden, Madelyn. You don't own it." Adam pointed out. "But look, there's a 'Closed for Maintenance' sign. We could put that by the gate, if you like."

"No," said Juliette. "Let strangers come in, let them see."

She spun around and her light summer dress swirled up in a wide circle of cloth like a toreador's cloak. "Maddy can be like the woman in *'En robe de parade - Samain'* and you can be the indiscreet man, Adam."

"Juliette, is that another of your poems? You two, you have the advantage over me, I'm feeling all left out." Maddy pouted, knowing full well she wouldn't be left out at all.

Adam laughed. "We'll need to find a little wall to cast your shadow against, you've got the flowing skirt already."

"See, you know exactly what Juliette's on about. Do I need to keep an eye on you two?"

"I thought you already were," replied Adam.

"Ah ha, Mister Cain, you've spotted the method in my madness." Maddy's eyes sparkled, she was going to enjoy herself this afternoon with her two new pets.

"More the madness in your method, Madelyn. But this place, you surprise me. I didn't think you so peaceful."

"I'm not always a woman in a hurry, Adam. Sometimes, I like a still place." She remembered his eyes holding hers when she fingered herself and came in their first meeting place, his quiet intensity anchoring her exhibition.

"Where are we?" asked Juliette.

"The Japanese Gardens," replied Adam. "It's one of my favourite places. Quite close to perfection."

Maddy heard his words, his deliberate choice of phrase, and was delighted. "Yes, perfection's very close, isn't it? I wonder if we'll find it." She kissed him lightly on the lips. "Come on, let's show Juliette."

"The trick, Juliette, is to go slowly, turn every corner with wide open eyes, and stop." Adam stopped walking, just before the entry arch. "See what I mean?"

Juliette saw a gateway in front of her, with two wooden doors opening inwards towards the garden. Beyond, she saw a path, but could see nothing else, for it forked just past the entry gate, one path curving out of sight to the left, the other out of sight to the right. She understood the space immediately - choices to be made with a vista beyond; come back again and go the other way, another time, in another place.

She turned to see Maddy and Adam standing side by side behind her. "It's clever," she said, and walked on ahead of them, one of the rugs tucked under an arm.

Maddy looped her arm through Adam's, and they too stepped through the gate, content to follow Juliette as she explored. She came to the fork in the path, looked left, then right, then took three more steps down the right-hand path, and stopped. "That's gorgeous, really lovely."

In front of her lay a small lake with a low mound of an island closer to one end, and further on, curves of rock and reed along the edge of its shore, with several stone viewing platforms and a flat stone bridge. A family of ducks had made one of the platforms its own, scattering the rock with black and grey droppings. The parent ducks stood watch, the drake standing on a rock, while the fledglings lay together, lazing in the warm sun.

"Look, there's a turtle's head." Juliette pointed, and they could see the tiny eyes just above the waterline.

She took in a deep breath before turning again to Maddy and Adam. Her eyes were bright, her lips slightly parted, and she was delightfully young and fresh. She spread her arms wide.

"Undo some buttons," she said, "I want to feel the sun on my skin."

Adam, carrying the picnic hamper in one hand, with Maddy on his other arm, was encumbered, and couldn't easily do it. Maddy moved forward, dropping her rug on the ground, and undid the top three buttons of Juliette's dress, revealing the cleavage between her breasts, and the edges of her lacy cupped bra. She carefully arranged the collar to show Juliette's throat and the delicate lace of the choker.

Maddy stroked the length of Juliette's throat with two fingers. "Isn't she lovely?" she said, presenting Juliette to Adam, but making it clear whose she was.

"Very beautiful, Maddy. You're lucky to have found her."

"Do you know," Maddy replied, "I think she might have found me."

This time, Juliette put her arm through Maddy's, and the two women walked on. "Pick up the rug, there's a darling."

"Am I your slave, Madelyn?" asked Adam.

" If you want to be," she replied.

Juliette smiled, and leaned her head against Madelyn's shoulder. The sun felt lovely and warm on the bare skin of her arms. She inhaled the scent of her mistress, and wondered what would happen. Maddy did indeed like an orchestration.

Behind them, they heard Adam bend down to pick up the dropped rug, and the sound of crockery sliding in the picnic hamper. "Christ," they heard him mutter, "who packed this?"

"Ooh, that was me. Didn't I tighten the straps?" Maddy laughed, "I'm so forgetful."

"No, you're not, Maddy. I doubt you forget much at all."

"You're very probably right." She chuckled. "Where shall we go? Somewhere shady, I don't want to catch the sun on my perfect skin."

Adam's eyes creased with a smile.

"How about over there?" Juliette pointed to the far corner of a well-kept lawn where a small glade had been laid out, backed by willows and semi-enclosed by a circle of small shrubs and low bushes. A standing stone had been placed at the outermost edge to evoke a distant mountain, and by the entry to the glade a stone lantern stood watch. At night in Edo it would have been lit. Here, it was a ceremonial thing.

"A garden within a garden, that's just what we need," replied Madelyn.

Juliette ran ahead, spinning once as she darted across the lawn. The swirl of her dress lifted the cloth high, showing her thighs and the lacy edge of her knickers.

"Isn't she gorgeous?" Madelyn admired the girl.

"Yes, indeed," replied Adam. "She seems to do you good."

"She does, doesn't she? I'm quite taken by her. She's very like me when I was her age."

"That's not so long ago, Madelyn."

"You flatter me, Mister Cain."

"Just watching my Ps and Qs."

Maddy laughed, delighted with Adam's response. "Come on, you wonderful man. Let's have our picnic. Over there, I think, don't you?"

Adam followed her to a spot just in front of the rock. She took the two rugs, the first one thrown to her by Juliette, and laid them out, then lay down, stretching herself out. "My shoes, if you don't mind." She looked up at Adam, a glint in her eye.

"I imagine you have grapes, Madelyn," he said, drily, but knelt at her feet to undo the straps of her heeled sandals, carefully holding each foot as he did so.

"Go on, you might as well, while you're down there."

Adam took each toe with its shining red polished nail into his mouth, one by one, sucking hard on it, tasting her faint sweat, stretching the length of each foot with his hands. Madelyn sighed with pleasure. "Ooo, you delectable man," she whispered.

Juliette watched and, without a word, slipped her own sandals off and presented her feet to Adam for attention. She lay facing Maddy, and both women looked down at the man at their feet, before turning towards each other for a kiss. Juliette's hand crept up inside Maddy's tank top, fingers rolling the nub of her nipple up to a tight peak. Madelyn gently stroked the girl's hair, looking again at Adam as he caressed their feet.

"He's very good, isn't he?" she said, and Juliette smiled, twisting Maddy's nipple hard to give her a sharp pain. "Ohh, naughty girl, so are you."

"What else have you got to eat?" asked Adam, shifting himself up beside them, a thickness evident in his trousers.

"Did I say you could stop?" Madelyn smiled, waiting for his response.

"No, but you promised me a picnic, Madelyn."

"Adam, so fierce, so demanding. See, Juliette, I told you he could be wilful."

"You shouldn't tease him, Madelyn." Juliette grinned. "It's too easy."

"Juliette, you *are* naughty! Isn't she bad, Adam, teasing you like that?"

Adam looked at the two women, an inscrutable look on his face. "Hmm, a man on a stage with no script. I'd better just do as I'm told, then?" He turned to the picnic hamper as if to assert himself over something, at least."Something like that, but it's only a picnic, my darling," Madelyn replied, "not the end of the world."

"Madelyn, I expect with you, even the apocalypse would do as it's told."

She laughed. "Oh, Mister Cain, you flatter me. You know I wouldn't do that." She looked at him with pleasure in her eyes. "Come here, you beautiful man, you may kiss me if you like."

"Fuck me, Madelyn, only if I like?" He leaned in towards her. "What do I need to do, to please you?"

"Fuck me. But not now, Mister Cain, this is only our second date." She leaned in towards him. "I'm not fast, or forward, remember?"

Adam laughed, then kissed her hard on the lips, forcing his tongue into her mouth. She resisted him at first, then sucked his tongue into her mouth, holding her hand to the back of his neck. He pulled away, but she pulled him back, and they fought.

Juliette rolled out of their way, sat up and watched. She saw Adam's hand move up to Maddy's breast, the same nipple she'd pulled up tight and hard just a moment before, and imagined his big hand pushing pleasure into Madelyn's tit. Juliette scooped inside her bra, pressing against her own nipple, quickly circling her palm on the rod to bring her own quick pain. Her breasts ached, and low in her belly another ache echoed. Juliette wanted them both, and wanted them to want her. She squeezed her left breast hard against her chest, her heart, and watched them.

Maddy pushed Adam back, breaking their kiss. She waved her hand theatrically in front of her chest, to cool herself. "Goodness, Mister Cain, I'm quite hot all of a sudden. Is it just me?"

"It is getting warm, it's not just you." Juliette spread her arms wide. "Adam, you can undo some more buttons, if you like." She tilted her head, looking up at him coyly from behind her fringe.

"Only if I like, Juliette?" He moved towards the girl, and undid the button between her breasts.

"Adam, I'm sad. Don't you want to fuck me, too?" Juliette pouted, and was so adorable with it that Adam sat back, shook his head, and laughed again.

"You two! I've got no dignity left with the pair of you, have I?"

"Isn't that what you want, Adam, no dignity?" asked Maddy.

Adam smiled, said nothing, but leaned forward and methodically undid every button on Juliette's dress, all the way to the hem. He separated the two sides of cloth away from her body to reveal silken emerald underwear, perfectly chosen by Bonnard to contrast with the girl's skin and to match the green of her eyes. Having done so, he took the girl's waist gently in both hands, and helped her to her feet. She looked up at him for a moment, then kissed him on the cheek. Adam slowly brought his hands up inside the back of Juliette's dress to her shoulders, sliding the cloth away so it fell in a pool at her feet.

She took a step back, flipping her hair. "That's much better, thank you." She turned around once, so both Maddy and Adam could see. Her delicate lingerie both covered her and displayed her, at the same time.

Then, quite deliberately, she stuck her tongue out at Adam with a wicked look in her eye, just a girl. "Your turn."

With the same deliberation, she undid each button on Adam's shirt, exposing the silvering hair on his chest and a darker strip down the centre of his gut. Juliette pulled the shirt ends up from his pants, and in an echo of Adam's undressing of her, she slid her hands up his back, and pushed the shirt back from his shoulders to fall in a fold behind him. Her hands were small on his body.

"There. You can feel the sun on your skin, too. Isn't it luscious?" She took him suddenly by the hand and ran around the lawn outside their little glade, so the rush of the wind could sparkle on their skin.

Now Madelyn was the only one of the three fully dressed, but the tight press of her nipples against the top revealed her arousal and delight at seeing Juliette's lovely body and her delicate silk and lace, as well as Adam's bare chest and the satisfying ridge in his pants. She'd have to do something about that, remembering the length of him in her hands and in her throat. She'd find somewhere for that splendid cock, no doubt, but was content to wait for his fuck.

"Aren't you still hungry, Adam? All this running about, it's exhausting."

"Madelyn, you're not even moving."

"I know, it's all in my head. But isn't it wonderful, this garden? The beautiful flowers, all this life! Oh, look at me, now I'm chattering." She sat up, reaching for the hamper. "Juliette, darling, don't get cold. Cover yourself up if you want to."

"I don't want to, Maddy. I'm wearing too much as it is."

She stood in front of Adam, now seated beside Maddy with his legs stretched before him, the thickness on his thigh still evident. Juliette ran one foot down it, then planted her feet wide, standing over him. "Look up," she instructed, and Adam tilted his head up to look into her eyes. She smiled back at him, returning his gaze with her own soft eyes. "Hello, Adam, I didn't say hello before."

"Hell - "

"Ah ah ahh, don't talk. I just said look."

With the same deliberate slowness as before, when she'd undone the buttons on his shirt, Juliette reached behind her back and unclipped her bra, then cupped both hands over the delicate cups of the brassiere, hiding her breasts.

"My eyes, Adam. Look up." She saw his eyes narrow and a muscle in his jaw tighten, as he looked up at her face, away from her curves.

"Good boy."

Beside him, Madelyn took a quick intake of breath, and slowly shifted her legs apart. She kept watching Juliette, and began to slide her hand inside the split of her own skirt, up along her thigh.

Juliette stood motionless for a long count of ten, holding Adam with her eyes. She slowly took her hands away from her breasts, dragging the flimsy covering away. She lifted her finger, *ah ah ah, not yet,* and waited another long count.

"You may look." She released him, and gloried in Adam devouring her breasts with his eyes, craving her curves, wanting to suck her in. He reached his hands up to her breasts.

"No," she said, and stepped on his thigh with her foot, pressing her weight down on the thickness there. "I didn't say touch."

Madelyn, beside him, eased her legs further apart and slid her long fingers around the slide of her sex, to scent herself. She put those fingers to Adam's lips so he knew her arousal was there, and she fucked her fingers into his mouth for moisture, and his suck. She returned her fingers to her cunt and slowly started to slide, again. She kept watching Juliette, her eyes heavy lidded, her arousal thick and heavy.

Juliette was air and lightness, her slender, slight body standing over Adam, the nipples on her high breasts hard and tight. A delicate blaze of freckles scattered down over the top curves of her breasts, where she'd caught the sun in a bikini perhaps, or an open-necked shirt.

Adam licked his lips, his mouth dry. He gazed at Juliette's high breasts, and she saw the stillness in his eyes deepen, not so still any more, not so certain.

Juliette was certain. "My underwear. You may take them off, but..." and she cautioned him with her finger, again, "... you mustn't touch longer than necessary."

"But - "

"No sound," she insisted, and lifted her foot in warning.

Knowing that Adam's eyes were glued to her fingers now, Juliette slowly slid them down her body, curving them under the weight of her breasts, cupping them; then she caressed her ribs slowly, her sides and belly, feeling her own skin, languorously and seductively stroking her own flesh. Coming to the waist of her panties, she slid a finger in along the top of the cloth, and pulled the fine elastic tight, letting it go with a quick snap on her skin.

"Now you may," and she gave him permission.

Beside him, Maddy hissed in a breath. Her scent was rising now, her fingers dipping into her cunt, still very slowly, but she was wet enough now, just watching.

Adam took in a deep, shuddering breath and kneeled before Juliette, his cock a tight, constrained ridge sheathed against his thigh. He placed his fingers carefully on the sides of her knickers, easing the lacy waistband away from her skin. He began to pull the cloth down from her hips and carefully over the curve of her ass, careful not to touch her body, careful not to touch her.

"Do you want to touch me, Adam, as you pull my knickers down?" Juliette's voice was quite conversational, as if every day a man in a park undressed a woman, and pulled her knickers down. He nodded, but continued to ease the panties down, still careful not to touch her skin. "Maybe later," she said, lifting first one foot then the other, so that Adam could remove the cloth from her feet. "Not yet." She said it as if she were shopping, or waiting for a bus.

"Give the panties to me " instructed Maddy, holding out her hand. She put the cotton centre of the flimsy garment to her nose, breathing the faint trace of the girl in, before dropping her hand to her own sex once more, mixing her own arousal into the cloth.

Adam watched the exchange between the women, but remained kneeling before Juliette, gazing at her mound, her belly, wanting to touch her, but not permitted.

His cock was firm but constrained, and Maddy knew Adam would be frustrated, as he had been at the truck stop before she released him and gave him suck. She wondered what Juliette had in mind, the wicked girl, for this man at her feet. The more Maddy saw, the more she marvelled at the girl. Quite an imagination, and such concentration. She momentarily wondered if she should take pity on Adam and rescue him from himself - but whilst that cock wanted rock hardness, she knew that would never do. *Oh no, Mister Cain, I could never do that. Goodness me, how delicious, this waiting.* She eased her fingers around her clitoris, prepared to torment herself slowly while she watched.

"In the hamper, Adam, are some strawberries. I'd like some, please." Juliette released him from his worship, but didn't move.

She glanced across at Madelyn, who lovingly smiled back at her, her fingers slowly moving at her core, slowly working herself up from her own quiet place, watching the girl with delight. And with admiration; so very like herself. How *did* she find her, this Juliette?

Adam found the punnet of strawberries and brought them back to Juliette. She took one and fed it to him, crushing its soft flesh between her fingers until the juice ran over his lips, leaving a little sticky trail down his chin. She dabbed it up with her finger, then took another strawberry and put it between her teeth, and leaned towards him. Adam took his half of the sweet fruit into his mouth, and tasted the sweetness on Juliette's lips.

"Take one to Maddy," said Juliette, finding a sweet, ripe strawberry and placing it between his teeth. Adam took it to the other woman, who tasted the sweet fruit and tasted his lips, too.

"I didn't get grapes, Adam, but does the colour of the strawberries remind you of anything?"

"You may speak, Adam," said Juliette, as she sat down next to Madelyn.

"He won't need to," said Madelyn, "he's seen this colour before." She parted her legs to show Adam and Juliette the smooth slit of her sex, a dark shadow against the alabaster whiteness of her thighs. She separated her lips to reveal the redness of her cunt, and it was the same vivid redness as the strawberry between her fingers, the berry she slid along herself like the head of a cock. She remembered the calm look on

Adam's face when she'd displayed herself in the office, but didn't see that stillness now. He almost looked ... afraid.

Both women looked at Adam, and saw him clench his jaw, and grip the grass with his fingers. "Fuuck," he said, in a strangled voice, "so close to perfection, but I know I can't have it. Jesus, what do I need to do?"

"Go down on me, while Juliette watches. Then it's her turn, whatever she wants, whatever pleases her."

"What about me?"

"What about you, Adam? What more do you want?"

"Fuck. You. Her. Us"

"Us, Adam? Is there an 'us'? I didn't know there was an 'us.'" Maddy took a bite from the strawberry, breaking its skin and mingling its crushed, sweet flesh with her own sex juice. Adam gripped the ground again, and it was plain to see his cock was straining for freedom.

"You sound very impatient, darling. Hasty. I mean, you briefly reached first base just now, that's very sixteen, I admit. But really, Adam, you didn't expect the world and your oyster too, so soon? Surely not. You know I don't do that, Mister Cain, not so soon."

Maddy leaned forward and popped the strawberry into his mouth. "But Juliette here, she's her own girl. Perhaps if you're nice..."

"I think he wants *you,* Maddy. Does this mean I have to share?" Juliette admired the bulge of Adam's thigh, and reached out her hand to touch him. "I don't mind sharing. May I?" she asked Adam. "Can I?" she asked Maddy.

"Of course you can, darling. I'm still in the mood to watch."

She lay back, turning herself slightly to give herself better access to her centre. She eased back her lips and slid her forefinger into her cunt. Madelyn moaned with pleasure, and began to masturbate a little faster.

"Oh look," said Juliette. "People."

"How tiresome," replied Madelyn. "Make them go away. You know I don't like eyes."

Juliette got to her feet, grabbing her dress as she did so. As she walked across the lawn she made it quite obvious she was completely naked at first, but she slipped the dress on. Then she wrapped decorum about herself like a knot, and approached the small group of Japanese tourists, come to see a tiny piece of their home in a strange land.

She pointed back at Maddy and Adam, any details too far away to see, and said something. One of the men looked across and gave a short bow, then gathered the rest of the group before him, and took another path, taking them out of sight. Juliette raised her hand and fluttered her fingers in farewell.

As she came back across the lawn, she let go the cloth of her dress, and it flowed and followed her like an open cloak, revealing the sexy sway of her walk, the taut muscle of her thighs. Juliette rode a bicycle to keep fit, with a bell and a basket on the front.

"Apparently," she said, "we're a group of models re-enacting famous paintings, and we're waiting for our photographer."

"Clever girl," said Maddy, returning her fingers to her cunt and watching with low-lidded eyes.

"Adam, can you turn and face the other way. Angles, you know, for the photographer." Juliette grinned. Adam looked up at her looking down at him, a question in his eyes, but did as he was told.

Maddy moved too and raised one leg, giving him a wide open view of her sex and her flickering fingers there. He lay closer than before, and could smell her hot, metallic scent. He dared to put his fingers within reach of her hand, if she wanted to touch him.

"That's better, Mister Cain, much better. Slow is best, don't you think."

She didn't touch him, but opened herself up for his eyes. She closed her own, and kept up the slow weave of her fingers, from clitoris to labia lips and a long slide between. Her motion was almost hypnotic.

"More fruit, Adam?" Juliette asked. "I've got a lovely peach you might like." She knelt beside him, facing towards his feet. She didn't search in the basket. Instead, she leaned down, her breasts dropping beautifully for him to see, and she rolled up two turns of a cuff on his pants.

"There. Mr Eliot would be proud."

"Oh, Juliette, clever girl," whispered Maddy, and her eyes to see.

Juliette sat back up, and ran her hand up Adam's leg to rest her palm on his hardness, still constrained against his thigh. She looked back at him to see his eyes as she pressed her hand down hard, feeling the thickness of his cock under her palm, between her fingers. She saw something in his eyes, and shook her head, twice. She put her forefinger to her lip, sshhh, and her smile as she smiled down at him was kind.

"Don't say a word, Adam, not until I say."

Juliette undid the buckle of his belt, undid the button too. She spread the opening of his pants apart as far as it would go, but the spread of cloth was restrained by the zip. She looked at the clothing as if presented with some unsolvable problem, and ran her fingers, splayed wide, up Adam's gut, as if that movement would bring some strange alchemy to the scene, and dissolve the cloth like a dream.

Adam gasped, inhaling quickly, and Juliette found the sensitive place again. She leaned forward to investigate further, and the tips of her breasts grazed his skin. She got distracted by her own sensation and swayed over him some more, lightly dragging her nipples and breasts across his body.

Madelyn sucked in the sight of those breasts, and loved the way they hung down like raindrops, with their weight.

Adam sighed in his pleasure.

Juliette brought herself back to her problem, and slowly dragged down the zip as if it was a new invention, some miraculous thing, to spread apart Adam's hiding places. She slowly reached down inside his pants, delaying her discovery and delaying his release. Juliette wasn't cruel, she'd release him, but wanted to take her time. She always ate ice-creams slowly, so she could lick the melting bits from her fingers, and whenever she ate cake, it was always in little bits so it would last the longest time.

She remembered Bonnard and his slow delight, and wondered what he would think of this man. "Maddy, has Adam seen Bonnard? What did he think?"

"My darling, what a wonderful idea. I'd not thought of that. Goodness me, yes, I must arrange it."

"You'll like Bonnard, Adam, he's got such exquisite taste. He'll appreciate a man like you."

Juliette reached deeper inside Adam's pants, and found the hot heat of his cock. "Ohh Maddy, his cock is so very, very hot, you must feel it one day."

"I have, Juliette, before we got to the restaurant. I had it in my throat." Maddy remembered, softly.

"My God, no wonder you wanted my fingers, if you've not had this in your cunt yet."

Juliette leaned forward once again so her eyes were closer to Adam's centre, so she could see every slow revelation. She pulled his shaft sideways and up from his thigh, so it was still hidden by cloth, but able to straighten now. She felt it grow, and her hand was far too small.

She felt Adam's breath quicken, and felt a tentative touch of his hand to her thigh. She let him keep it there, and pulled his cock out further, revealing it now, straight up his belly.

"Fuck. Adam, that's nice, that's very, very nice." Juliette looked down in wonder, and took the big red cock end of his prick straight into her mouth, to eat that fruit and to feel the heat. At first she just mouthed his cock head, feeling a small movement as his shaft tried to bounce, but still the cloth constrained him; then she sucked, and sucked hard, pulling her teeth over the ridge of him, hearing him gasp.

"Fuck," he muttered, "that's good."

Juliette smiled around his head, and he must have felt that, as his fingers gripped her thigh.

She sucked on him, two hands now on his shaft, not moving, just feeling his thickness, his length, his heat. She reached in further, and cupped a palm around his balls, but the cloth of his pants was all too tight, and frustrated her.

So she released him from her suck, and remembered where she was. She crawled over Adam's body to Madelyn, and gave her the rich male taste mingled with her own, in a long, deep kiss. Maddy sucked the taste of him into her mouth, and returned the gift with a tongue fuck back into the girl's eager mouth. Adam's fingers gripped Juliette's flesh, hurting her, and she bit that sweet pain into Madelyn's lip. Then she let Maddy's mouth go, crawling back to Adam.

"I promised you a peach," she said, her voice low with lust, her mouth a hot, wet mess of Maddy's spit and her own, the taste of Adam all sucked away. "But first..."

She pushed the waist of his pants down, and Adam raised his ass to help her drag the constraints of the cloth away. At last his full length sprang free, angled up from his gut, bobbing now as it fully thickened and strained. Because his cock had been held tight for so long, the shaft was a deep purple red like a bruise, and his balls were big in her palm, high up to his body.

"That's a beautiful cock there, Adam. Very nice."

Juliette ran both her hands up his shaft, twisting around his length. She stretched out her fingers to measure him, from the tips of her thumb to her forefinger, but her span wasn't wide enough. "Very fucking nice. Very long. I like it."

"And perfectly straight," whispered Madelyn, "see how it's perfectly straight."

"You don't often see that," said Juliette, moving down his body for another inspection. For several minutes she lay beside Adam, her head facing his feet, his cock in her hand and her lips moving sideways up and down the shaft. And all the time she kissed him there, she held Maddy's eyes, and the two women devoured each other's eyes and minds as they worshipped the cock between them.

Madelyn's fingers were still deep in her cunt, building up her pleasure from watching, watching, and knowing she'd fuck that cock soon. She took Adam's hand, and placed his fingertips against her perfect thigh. "Soon, Adam, I promise."

Juliette said, "I promised you a peach, a juicy, juicy peach." She flipped the cloth of her dress, opened wide at the front, over Adam's head and onto the ground behind him, and she kneeled over him, her thighs on each side of his body, facing his feet. Spread wide, her sex was split right in front of his eyes; and with the faint down of her hair, very light along her lips, and her lips all tidy and neat, there it was, her succulent peach.

Adam brought his hands up to Juliette's ass cheeks and spread her wider, opening her up to his eyes. And his mouth, for she sat back onto his mouth and face, grinding herself down on him, forcing her sex over his face, before easing herself up so he could breath. Holding her cunt wide with his fingers, Adam fucked his tongue up into her.

With a high moan, almost a cry, "Ohh, fuck, yes," Juliette fell forward and took his cock into her mouth and repeated the suck, this time deeper, fucking down his shaft with her mouth stretched, her spit shining.

"God, fuck, that's exquisite," whispered Madelyn, soaking up the sight of the girl who'd taken her cunt so quickly viciously deep with her fingers, now taking that perfect cock, just as she had, in her mouth. "Make him come, Juliette, so I can see. We'll lick him clean together."

From where she lay, Maddy couldn't see Adam's mouth on Juliette's cunt, just the girl's tightening thighs, her straining legs, and every now and then a quiver. She began to imagine her own cunt there on his face, with Juliette in front of her, impaled on Adam's long cock, their breasts mashed together, fucked and fucking and fucked. She masturbated faster, eager to match the arousal of the couple in front of her. Madelyn kept her eyes open, and watched.

Juliette stroked Adam's cock faster, judging the speed of his breathing and his efforts in her cunt. She knew she was bringing him closer, closer to coming, sweet fuck in her mouth, and she stopped...

...she stopped and was still, her body motionless on his face, her mouth motionless around the head of his cock, she stopped. And felt his cock pulse once, twice, and she gripped his shaft tight, and with her other hand, pulled his balls down away from his body to stop the come, to stop the surge. Juliette held herself still to let Adam catch himself, and his mouth breathed hot breath into her sex as he held himself back.

"Good boy," she breathed, her voice a soft reward. "Me, first. Fuck me."

And Juliette held Adam still in her hands, as again he licked and sucked on her cunt. She shifted her body over him, so he could better lick her clitoris and rise her up, swirling his tongue around her tingling nerves. She poised herself, her thighs taut and trembling, slightly higher so he couldn't tongue fuck her, just lick her, and he moved one hand up to a breast. Her nipple was ice tight and rigid, and he twisted the piercing bar with his fingers, stabbing sensation into her tit which immediately connected with her clit.

Beside them, Madelyn's breath grew ragged, and Juliette heard the soft slick of her fingers, the same sound she'd heard in Bonnard's shop and in the toilet cubicle, as Maddy frigged herself. Juliette knew some triggers now, with Maddy, and...

"Maddy, Maddy, three fingered slut three fingers fast and deep, three hundred bucks you're so cheap. Three of us now, but I've got him. Come first, lying there breathing fast," Juliette started up a sing-song song for Maddy, "...fingering yourself coz I've got his cock and it's my cunt on his face and you want it on yours..."

And she was crooning for Adam too, to double his swirl on her clit because she was close, so close...

"Oh fuck, Maddy, look at me, I'm..."

With a high squeal of ecstasy, Juliette came, her hand gripping Adam's cock in a tight clench. Seeing her come toppled Maddy over her edge, and she came too, with long, aching sigh that ended with a sob, a low moan.

The three of them were momentarily frozen in time, caught in the moment. A photographer could have gone click.

Juliette broke the stasis by easing herself off Adam. Still holding his prick, she turned and moved down his body. She started up her stroke once more, and if anybody had chanced upon the lawn they'd have seen her hand on his cock.

Juliette said, "Adam," and he turned his eyes to hers, and with a steady, constant gaze, Juliette pulled his soul up into her eyes. She watched him as she urged him up, watched him as he struggled to stay with her eyes, watched him as he couldn't.

Adam's eyes flickered closed, and with a last, futile reach for her skin, Juliette urged him up and he came, with three powerful throbs of his shaft, and three long streams of cum jetted up and splashed on his chest.

Madelyn moaned at the sight of his pleasure, and the gift he gave her. She rose from her languid recline and crawled to his body. Juliette moved up beside her, and between them, they licked his flesh clean, like two cats finding cream.

Maddy moved further up to kiss Adam, giving him the taste of his cum to remember her by.

"Not yet, Mister Cain, not yet."

Adam lay naked before them, his hands twitching with after-tremors of sexual release, but he shook his head side to side several times as if to say no. The women watched him.

"He's not quite ready," said Juliette. "He doesn't want you enough, not yet. He should have said no to me."

"But darling, how could he have resisted you, you're so lovely. And your little peach, that's so very sweet." Her laugh, when she said it, was delightful.

"He shouldn't have, Maddy, not if he really wants you." Juliette was really quite serious.

"When he needs me, Juliette. That's when I want him, not before." So was Maddy, very serious.

"It's your choice, darling," she said, with her finger on Adam's jaw. "Get dressed, there's a good boy."

Adam remained silent, but did as he was told.

Later, Madelyn walked through the garden holding Juliette and Adam by the hand. A curious observer would have said how beautiful they all were, walking by.

The Viewing Room

"Adam darling, are you free Tuesday evening? There's something I'd quite like you to see."

...

"Of course I'll be there ... oh, silly boy, don't think that."

...

"Juliette? You'll see. Well, yes, you will see, that's rather the point."

...

She laughed. "Oh no, Mister Cain, I don't do that."

...

She chuckled at his reply. "I'll send a car, about seven. Don't dress up."

Maddy hung up the office phone, smiling. Once again she'd denied Adam access to her private number. Now that the project work was done, he was fast running out of reasons to call the front desk to be put through to her office. Maddy suspected he would soon stop doing so, before Theresa began to shake her head. Adam would not countenance that. Theresa would miss the attention, though, that twenty second glow.

Maddy sat at her desk a moment longer, quietly thinking, before realising she was tapping two fingernails on the rim of her coffee cup, empty in the morning. Damn the man. *Damn Theresa*, she thought. *I want those twenty seconds for myself.* Astonished at her out-of-character reaction, she pulled up the meeting room booking page and blocked out MS3 for an hour, just after lunch. She had to pick up some dry-cleaning, or she'd have booked an earlier slot. She needed to get herself back in control with some Maddy time.

On the way out, an hour later, she smiled at Theresa at the front desk. "Just going out to pick up some dry-cleaning. Won't be long."

"Oh, you should have said. I'd have picked it up for you on my break." Theresa smiled back at her. "I wouldn't mind."

Madelyn looked at the girl for a long moment, before turning towards the lifts to press the button there. She faced the doors and smoothed down the tight cloth of her skirt, so that Theresa could see there was no panty line. Maybe Adam and I are the same, after all, she thought, and stepped into the lift, pressing the button for the ground floor. As she turned to face the reception desk, Maddy saw Theresa's head was tilted down, deliberately not looking back. The girl's fingers were touching her throat, surprised at the quick heat, perhaps.

Maddy smiled. Maybe Theresa would like to take notes in the meeting space some time. Junior staff needed mentors, the corporate policies said so - Maddy would know, she'd written that one. It was nearly time for the bi-annual policy review, perhaps she did need a Strategic Projects Consultant after all. She laughed at the silly thought. She didn't need an excuse to see Adam; he was reason enough, by himself.

"Adam, thanks for coming. Short notice, I know, but opportunity knocking and all that. Please, come in."

Madelyn welcomed Adam into the room, through a door opening off the same arcade corridor as Bonnard's shop. She watched him quickly scan the place, which was nondescript. The only clues to its purpose were a single hook firmly anchored to the exact centre of the ceiling, a chair of simple design, its legs incongruously painted red, placed beneath the hook, and a thin Japanese style mattress on the floor, neatly fitted into a corner. A series of enclosures and shelves were fitted to the wall above the mattress, making a matrix of geometrically designed spaces, too big for books. Adam ran his finger along a smooth edge on one of the timber enclosures, then raised a quizzical brow towards Maddy.

"Patience, darling. It's your turn to watch." She met his gaze. "Through here," she said, and ushered Adam through to a small room with two arm-chairs side by side, facing a wide window which looked into the space they'd first entered. "It's mirrored glass; we can see them, they see themselves."

"They, Madelyn?"

"You'll see," Maddy replied. "It's all about you seeing, watching, this time. I've had my turn, in the garden. A drink, can I get you a drink? Wine, spirits?"

"A red, thanks. Burgundy, if you have it."

"Of course I do. I won't be long." Maddy left the room, leaving Adam to make himself comfortable in one of the chairs.

She was deliberately gone a few extra minutes, making him wait, thinking he would start wondering what was about to happen. But when she returned, a single glass of wine in her hand like blood, she found him sitting with an enigmatic stillness, a quiet contemplation on his face, as if the only company he needed was his own.

She looked down at Adam, silently studying him, waiting for him to acknowledge her return to the room, waiting for his attention. He slowly stirred, as if he'd been far, far away and had only just arrived back. "Madelyn," he said, softly.

"Yes, Adam?" She whispered too.

"Nothing. I just like the sound of your name. Madelyn. Do you have a second name?"

"Jane. Madelyn Jane." Maddy gave him the glass. She rarely gave anybody her middle name, and not many asked.

"Jane. That's my sister's name." He smiled up at her. "I don't see her often. I never really did. She's five years older than me, and left home when I was twelve. She was seventeen."

Maddy wasn't quite sure why he did the maths on their relative ages, it being a simple sum, but sensed a lingering something in his words. "Best you call me Madelyn, then. I'm not your sister." She sat on the arm of the chair, and realised she wanted to be near him. "Or Maddy. I like it when you call me both names."

"Miss Maddy, Mistress Madelyn, is that it?"

"Do you want that?" Her heart, surprisingly, thumped, not knowing the answer and almost fearing the question, even from her own lips.

Adam took her hand in his and circled her wrist with his fingers, where she still wore his watch, taken from him at the garden. "I don't know, Madelyn, I really don't know." He tapped the watch face with his finger. "But I seem to be giving you parts of myself, bit by bit, don't I?" He looked up into her eyes, and she saw the stillness there, once again. "And I don't seem to be wanting them back. Why is that, do you think?"

Madelyn looked at him for a moment, then gently put a hand to his cheek, surprised at her own tenderness. She felt a slight added weight on her palm as he lay his head lightly on it, as if it were a small pillow. "I think," she said, slowly, "that you want Maddy the girl in the street, as well as Madelyn who drives a fast car."

"Which one are you?"

"Both. Bloody infuriating, isn't it?" Maddy smiled, placing both hands on his cheeks and turning his head to face her. "Can we just keep going, and one day I'll decide who I am?"

"That won't work. I'll want the other version, once you decide who you are. The perfect, unobtainable you." Adam touched her cheek, to see if it was warm, perhaps, or porcelain cold.

She laughed. "Mister Cain, must you be so difficult?"

"Maddy, you wouldn't enjoy me half so much if I gave up without a fight."

"God, you're delicious. Fight me, and find out, why don't you?" Maddy's eyes sparkled with joy.

"I just might, Madelyn, I just might." Adam taunted her. "But not tonight."

"Are you denying me, Mister Cain?"

"Do you know, Madelyn, I just might be." Adam teased her some more.

"Ooo, I love it when you play hard to get," she replied, kissing him lightly on the lips and stroking her fingers lightly on the back of his neck. "Not tonight. You sound like me, Mister Cain."

"Only the best, Madelyn, only the best."

"Good boy. Delight is like a fine wine, I find. The longer you keep it corked, the better it tastes."

"Can I read your label in the meantime?" he asked, taking a taste from his glass. "You know I like a bold red."

"I thought you liked a delicate, fruity white, with a hint of peach and a taste of honey."

"Ah yes, Juliette, she really was delightful, wasn't she? I'm assuming she's your plaything tonight, if I'm the silent observer? Will she know I'm here?"

"It won't matter if she does," said Maddy, getting up from the chair.

"Bound and gagged, is that it?"

"Something like that. Go in when you're ready, if you want to. I'll leave it entirely up to you."

"Another one of your tests, Maddy?

"If you like," she replied. "Don't fail. Give something else up."

Her eyes suddenly went dark, and a shot of ice hit behind her nipples, shocking them hard in a second.

Juliette came into the display space wearing a floor length gown which completely concealed her body, her head obscured by a hood. She had arrived earlier and been met by Roshi-san, an artist Madelyn knew through Bonnard. Like Bonnard, Roshi prepared as any artist does, with care and tenderness, and intense concentration.

Madelyn, who didn't know those moods, or if she did they weren't upon her, left them alone in a small room. She sat now beside Adam in the second chair, remaining silent, wanting to observe his reaction to the ritual about to unfold.

Earlier, she'd asked Juliette, "Are you ready, are you prepared? Are you sure?"

"I'm sure, Madelyn. I want this moment, it's mine."

Madelyn admired the girl, and envied her the journey she would take and the place she would find on her arrival. But Adam was here, so Madelyn hoped for something different, a new, quiet force in the room.

The viewing window was sound-proofed, and the only sounds Madelyn heard were her heart inside her ears and the slow breath of Adam beside her. She watched a blue pulse on his wrist where his watch had been strapped before she took it. It was a slower beat than hers and grounded her, like her two fingers usually did. She smiled at the thought - his silence calms me more than sex, how can that be? She studied his fingers, and imagined them parting her lips, slowly entering her sex, gently fucking her, and all the while his other hand held the glass of wine. She looked up to his face, but he was looking out at the scene before them.

Every now and then he took a small taste from the wine-glass, and she imagined kneeling before him, her breasts dropping with their own small weight, pushing herself back onto his fingers, two fingers to open her up, three fingers in a longer fuck, his thumb and little finger like a wedge, hard against the bones of her cunt. Maddy crossed her legs and angled her body towards Adam in the chair, a long leg stretching towards him, her foot not quite touching his leg.

Adam looked back at her, and his eyes were dark like clouds gathering before a storm. He gazed at her for a long while, silently, then turned his eyes back towards the other room, watching Juliette instead of her.

Maddy quivered, her body twitching once with her silent arousal. She clenched muscles deep in her core, tightening her ass, and shuddered again. She tightened once more, and her breasts ached and her nipples were hard spikes piercing behind her chest. Maddy wanted the fill of a fuck, but she'd wait... the longer you keep it corked, the better it tastes. She felt a ripple of pleasure course through her body, heightened by her denial of self and her waiting.

She saw Adam's slow arousal from watching the next room, a shift of his thighs and his blue pulse beating slightly faster. Enjoying the sensations in her own body, she turned her attention away from Adam for the time being, and saw Juliette through the window.

The girl was naked now, kneeling on the thin mattress. Roshi was beside her, dressed in a simple black tunic, a long length of rope in his hand. Juliette was facing away from the viewing window, so Maddy could see the cello curve of her back and buttocks, her flesh lightly dimpled under her skin.

Roshi had already tied Juliette's hands behind her back with an elegant knot, and was looping the rope around the girl's torso. He'd completed a four strand bind around her upper back and breasts, and was slowly circling another band at her waist. His hands were slow caution on the girl's skin, making sure the ropes were properly layered and looped.

Roshi helped Juliette stand, her legs slightly apart, and he passed the ropes between her legs and around one thigh.

"It's beautiful work, but she's not restrained," said Adam. "She could wear the ropes under a pretty dress, and no-one would know. She can ease her hands free. She can walk."

"She would know," said Madelyn, turning to Adam. "What would you do?" she asked, watching Adam's face for the things he wouldn't say.

"Bind her helpless, if that's what she wants," Adam replied. "Give her release, if she wants it. Frustrate her, if she wants that. Torment her, even."

"Would you fuck her?"

"If she wanted fucking."

"And if she didn't?" Maddy prompted.

Adam turned to Madelyn and studied her face. She held his gaze.

"Well? Would you fuck her if she didn't want you to?" She insisted on an answer.

"No, Madelyn, I wouldn't fuck her. I don't take what's not given."

"Even if she's made available?" Maddy wanted to know where Adam really stood on this.

"Available doesn't mean given, Maddy. She's not yours to give."

Maddy considered this, and knew Adam was right. She remembered Juliette's words, "But you're not paying. I'm volunteering."

She continued looking at Adam, and understood him better. "Prove it to me. Go ask Roshi to display her, so you could fuck her if she wanted you to." She looked at Adam, her eyes dark. "Or take her, if she doesn't."

"For fuck's sake, Maddy. No always means no."

"Prove it." Maddy was relentless. "She's desirable, isn't she?"

"She is, yes. Okay, I'll prove it." Adam got to his feet, but before he left the room he leaned down and took Maddy's face in his hands. He kissed her, hard, on the lips. "But I won't take her, not even for you. No matter how much you want me to."

Madelyn felt a slow chill creep over her, and a strange, dark delight. She might have to give herself to this man, after all, if he wouldn't take her. She knew they weren't talking about Juliette.

After Adam left the viewing chamber, Maddy undid the buttons of her blouse and looked down at her small breasts. She took her left nipple between the fingers and thumb of her right hand and pinched it hard, enjoying the short jab of pain. She then caressed both breasts in the palm of her hands, loving the tight weight of them as she pressed her breasts against her chest. She closed her eyes, and her breasts felt bigger, her whole sensation focussed there like a stranger's eyes.

She stirred, and glanced into the room, seeing Adam approach Roshi with a respectful bow. They exchanged words, and Roshi nodded. She watched Adam approach Juliette, saw her look up at him, and saw her smile as she said yes.

Maddy smiled to herself, and she stood to undo the waist of her skirt, which fell away from her long legs into a circle of cloth on the floor. She shrugged the blouse off, too. She stood naked, other than a pair of black stockings high on her thighs. Maddy ran her hands down the hard flatness of her belly, dipping two fingers over her clitoris and easing her lips apart. She was wet already, and breathed her own scent in.

Maddy sat back down in the chair and took the glass of wine in her hand. She turned her eyes to the room.

Adam stood back, giving Roshi space and time to contemplate how to tie Juliette so that she was truly restrained, and at the same time, exposed. Maddy watched, and the silence of her small room lent a disembodied air over the proceedings, as if the three players were actors on some silent movie screen, their movements played out in dumb-show.

Juliette lay on her back, her thighs splayed, exposing her sex wide open, the deep redness of her inner lips clearly showing; a pomegranate, not a peach. Roshi bent her left calf against her thigh, and coiled rope around the bent limb, immobilising the leg. He repeated the coil and tie on Juliette's right leg, and the girl was tied and spread, unable to move.

Maddy leaned forward to better see the girl's exposed cunt, dipping deep into her own sex for pleasure. She heard soft, whimpering moans and realised they were her own.

Roshi stepped away from Juliette, and moved to the chair in the middle of the room, his artistry complete. As the rigger, his careful watching eyes remained on the girl. He acknowledged Adam's presence, but wouldn't look away.

Adam looked towards Maddy in her silent room, then went to Juliette and kneeled by her head, bending low, his mouth near Juliette's ear. Maddy assumed he was negotiating boundaries with the girl, and wondered whether she would have done the same, or just taken her. She really didn't know.

Adam though, he caressed Juliette's cheek with his fingers, and Maddy saw the way the girl leaned her head towards his hand, resting her cheek on it. Maddy saw it was the same subtle movement that Adam had made earlier, when he too had rested his head on her hand. She wondered if it was a conscious or an unconscious thing, as it was barely perceivable. Madelyn recognised trust when she saw it, and thought it precious.

She watched them kiss, and saw how Juliette, even though she was tied and bound, yearned upwards for Adam's lips, hungry for the man, hungry for his mouth, to be eaten. There was nothing hidden there, no question; the girl wanted Adam. Madelyn ached as she saw how tenderly Adam held Juliette's head in both his hands, cradling her head as he kissed her.

Sweet god, will he be as gentle with me, when finally he kisses me like that? Madelyn thrust her fingers inside herself, finding her own arousal, finding a place where she could close her eyes and not see the other pair as they made love.

Maddy opened her eyes, immediately chasing that thought - she wanted to see Adam and Juliette make love, because she recognised love when she saw it; even if for only five minutes. Maddy liked the girl and wished it a longer time, as a gift; but she knew that really, she wanted love for herself. For the first time in a very long time, Maddy was no longer in control of her emotions, and was no longer sure what to do. She had deliberately invited Adam into her life; maybe this was why. She wanted what he brought to her, and what he took away.

Adam placed Juliette's head carefully onto the mattress and moved down between her legs. His fingers, which had been gentle on her cheek, were now just as gentle on the insides of her thighs. Maddy remembered how soft the skin was on Juliette's inner thighs, and seeing the deep pulse near her groin where the skin was so very delicate and pale, quickly beating. She imagined it flickering now, like a little bird's quick heart, beating fast.

Juliette, bound, could only shake her head as if saying no, but Maddy could see she was talking, crying out with pleasure, arching her neck in rigid ecstasy; and Maddy knew Juliette was crying out yes, yes, yes, sweet fuck, yes; and it was her own voice Maddy heard, as she peaked herself up and came, nearly sobbing; watching, watching, watching the girl as Adam fucked into her with his fingers, watching how Juliette arched herself up to his thrust as if the ropes could barely hold her body from him. Maddy watched Juliette come on Adam's fingers, his fuck given swiftly, pleasuring the quivering girl.

Then, oh god, Maddy cried out, as Adam did it again and took the girl once more. This time, Juliette shook her head from side to side, but Adam stilled the movement with his mouth on hers as he fucked her with his fingers, and his fingers were enough. Juliette came again, and her body slumped onto the mattress. Adam placed her there like a baby into a cradle.

Madelyn wrapped her arms around herself for warmth and comfort, her feet up on the chair, her knees held tight to her chest. She watched Adam care for the girl, and waited for him to come back to her.

She saw Adam say something to Roshi, and saw the rope-master speak in reply, then get up and leave the room. Madelyn watched as Adam carefully released the knots and untwisted the rope from Juliette's body, and she watched the girl stretch and turn, still limp and loose on the mattress. Adam got up, and came back with water in a bottle, and Juliette's long gown.

Maddy watched as Adam dressed the girl, and knew it was a natural thing for him to do. She could tell from watching that he had children of his own who had once been small. He sat back in the corner of the room and opened his arms for Juliette, who crawled to him, her arms and legs weak and shaking. Maddy watched as Juliette curled herself small in Adam's arms, one hand slipped under his shirt to rest on his chest over his heart, the other curled small in a tiny fist between her breasts; her thumb almost moving to her mouth. Her fingers flexed against his heart like a kitten's paw bringing up milk from a mother, settling down into a sleep.

Maddy saw how Adam cradled the girl's head to his shoulder, and how he wrapped his arms around her. Madelyn had never seen such a gentle man, and she waited.

After ten minutes, Juliette stirred from her trance and looked around, as if to discover where she was. She reached up for Adam's face and touched his cheek, and her eyes were huge. Maddy saw him bend down to kiss her, a simple kiss on the lips. Juliette wriggled off his lap and sat cross-legged for a minute.

After long moment, Adam got to his feet and helped Juliette stand. She was a little wobbly, but refused Adam's help as she walked slowly to the door from which she'd entered the room in the first place. She held her head high.

Adam watched her go, watched the door close behind her. He then moved to the mirrored glass and looked directly at Madelyn, and would have seen himself. Madelyn saw him mouth the words, "Come here, come out here."

She got to her feet, and went to him.

"You didn't fuck her," she said.

"I didn't need to. She was content with my fingers, and not being able to move. She said, 'If fingers were good enough for Madelyn, they're good enough for me.' She said to use three fingers."

Madelyn nodded. She understood that. "You cared for her, afterwards. That was lovely to see. You let her be small in your arms."

Adam smiled, and Maddy sensed some distant memory in the darkness of his eyes, and thought it wasn't the first time he'd been a safe place for a girl who slept.

"Can I sleep in your arms one day?" Maddy asked. "Like Juliette just did. I'd like that."

"I thought you didn't do that, Madelyn."

"A woman can change her mind," she replied.

Adam looked at her with a wry smile. "I reckon you made your mind up a while ago, Maddy, you just forgot to tell yourself."

She laughed, and moved towards him, placing one long leg between his legs and her bare sex against his thigh. Her hands went up inside his shirt at the back, then she ran her fingers down his spine.

"Take this off," she said, and bunched his shirt up and over his head. "Lie down. You've been kind. Now it's my turn."

Adam lay down, and without fuss or delay, Maddy undid the buckle of his belt, undid his fly, and slid his trousers and briefs down his legs, peeling them off his feet. He lay naked on the mattress where Juliette had lain.

His cock quickly grew rigid, straight and thick up his gut, his arousal undiminished.

"You must be horny as fuck, after Juliette," said Maddy, lying down with her head on his chest, gazing down at Adam's shaft. She shifted down his body, took the cock-head in her mouth, hollowed her cheeks, and sucked.

She lay at right angles to him, stretched long on the mattress. Adam could reach her back, and tried to touch the taut globes of her ass, but she moved away so he couldn't reach her there.

"Just you, your cock," she said, before engulfing his shaft once again. Adam brought his hand back to the top of her spine, resting there, touching her. Maddy turned her mind to his pleasure, and didn't think about herself at all. Trance like, her existence centred on Adam's cock, its length, the cool weight of his balls, the blood hot heat of his shaft. She slowed her suck, and took the length of him into her hands, and began to slowly stroke.

She knew enough of Adam now, his transcendent places, to know he would give his pleasure up slowly, let her take him to a higher place. She didn't want quick release, she'd save her cunt for later, and she'd fuck him slowly when their time was ready; but now it was the sweet joy of hearing his breath catch, feeling his hand grip her skin as she paused...

... And began to move again, slowly stroking.

Maddy closed her eyes, and felt the velvet smoothness of his cock head on her lips, the heat of him on her cheek. She pressed the tip of her tongue into the little slit on his head, and smiled to herself when he gasped. Oh fuck, his breath was more and more ragged, and her nipples and breasts throbbed with her own delight, but it was the cock in her mouth, the hot cock in her hand that mattered, his hot shaft stroked back and forth. Adam arched his back, gripped her neck...

...and Maddy stopped, and waited, and breathed hot breath to cool his heat, and didn't move and didn't move, and she found his still place...

... and began again to move within it, finding his stillness and his heat, and she matched her breath to his, and his cock became the centre of her existence, the only thing in the room, and Maddy loved that long cock and tasted its flesh with delight, and she took him to the back of her throat and fucked him down to her depths, and Maddy took his cock and heard his slow moan and oh sweet fuck she made the man hers...

... and took him into her mouth and her lips and with her small teeth bit him gently and his hand gripped her skin and his other hand couldn't help it, he held her head and held her there but she didn't need to be held because his cock was in her mouth and names didn't matter anymore because he was getting so close so close so close...

... she didn't stop stroking this time, didn't speed up either, and in the one moment between this one and the next she knew she knew she knew that he wouldn't stop couldn't stop and in a still place in a silent room her man made no noise but spilled his seed into her mouth, slow surges of thick pleasure as he gave himself up to her and spilled hot luscious semen into her mouth and she swallowed him down swallowed him down and with a smile on her face she had him, he'd given himself up to her; and she smiled, such joy. In this moment the man was hers, given up...

... And slowly Maddy came back to her senses, and wiped her mouth. She cupped her hands lovingly over the softening heat of his shaft and his tight balls, and ever so gently she moved her long body next to his, and lay herself on top of him, the heat of his prick thick against her belly. She lay upon him, and Adam put his arms around her and was big and still and quiet and held her in his arms.

Maddy kissed him, and gave him his own taste for his lips.

"Hello, Adam," she whispered. "Was that nice?" She smiled, and snuggled her head to his shoulder, kissing the soft hollow of skin on his throat.

"Maddy," he said.

Maddy smiled. She was the girl in the street, and she had him, now.

"Madelyn."

Madelyn smiled. She was the woman in a fast car. "Soon, my darling. Can't you wait?"

Adam's Apartment

"Adam," said Juliette, "is that you?"

...

"Can I see you?"

...

"Sooner would be nice. I wanted to thank you."

...

She smiled at his response. "No, it was my pleasure."

...

She laughed, and her eyes lit up. "Both our pleasures, then."

...

"Your place. I'd prefer your place. I'm in a group-house and it's, well, messy..."

...

"Filthy, actually. One room is full of ski gear that's only been used once. I've given up nagging. I keep telling him, sell the bloody stuff if you're not using it!

...

"What can I bring?"

...

"Apart from myself. I can drop by somewhere on the way... okay, that sounds good."

...

"No, she doesn't know. We don't have her number, remember."

After the call, Juliette opened a beautiful box containing another set of Bonnard's lingerie. She didn't know Adam's apartment, but thought the dark blue might be best. It would match his eyes. She'd sensed a vanity in the man, and thought he'd like that.

"Juliette, come in, make yourself at home. Here, let me."

She gave Adam the carry bag from a gourmet deli nearby, and he took it through to the kitchen. She followed, dropping her shoulder bag onto the bench, with her car keys on top. She went to him, reaching up on her toes for a kiss, affectionate for him, a pretty girl in a plain cotton dress.

He didn't compliment her with words, and she didn't think he would. Adam had a way of noticing beautiful and elegant things around him that came from the corners of his eyes. Juliette had seen it briefly at the restaurant, and more closely in the garden, that crease of appreciation. She saw it now, and smiled back, accepting the recognition. She liked being noticed, and why not? She was the kind of girl people gazed at, only then realising what they were doing. Juliette liked their spontaneous smiles, they were like the sun coming out on dappled leaves, after rain.

"Look around, if you like. I'll put these on some plates, and we can sit outside, watch the sunset." Adam turned to cupboards and drawers, getting out plates and glasses. "Can I get you a drink?"

"Just water, for now," replied Juliette, to remind them both of the last time he got her water.

"Cold or tap?"

"Fridge'd be nice, thanks."

Adam poured her a glass from a cold bottle and she took it, feeling the coolness against her fingers. She turned from the kitchen to study the living space, and saw its elegant symmetry.

A wide, comfortable couch faced a wide-screen TV, but instead of the usual black and silver boxes and skinny speakers tucked alongside, she saw a set of unfamiliar equipment with black lumps of metal and what looked like small light bulbs in a row across the front. A turntable sat upon its own shelf. Juliette had never seen speakers like the ones in the room, a pair of tall, wide slabs, each with two speakers exposed to the air. Intrigued, she opened a glass fronted cabinet, and saw shelves of LP covers; hundreds of albums, she thought.

"God, that's a lot of records. How does this all work?" She thought of her little collection of CDs and her iPod full of downloads. She pictured herself on the bus with white dangling cords from her ears, and guessed Adam never listened to music that way. She angled her head to read some of the titles; most she'd never heard of, but she vaguely knew some of the bands. His CD collection was equally large, but she recognised more titles, more band names, as most of the albums were newer.

"Just a sec, and I'll show you."

But by the time he'd finished in the kitchen, Juliette had discovered another room, a smaller one. Two walls were completely filled with floor-to-ceiling books, and opposite the door, a long window overlooked the parkland below, a comfortable chair looking out. She ran her fingers along the spines of books, taking in the wide range of subject matters, their vastly different ages. She could lose herself in here for a very long time.

"This is amazing," she said. "Have you read them all?" She turned to Adam, who stood by the door, watching as she discovered his world of words and pictures.

"Most of them, yes. There's a few that I might have bought on a whim, that I haven't got to yet." He crossed to a shelf of older books, and ran his finger across their spines. "These are some I had as a teenager, these a bunch from uni. I keep buying books, and inherited a lot from my father."

Juliette stood by his side, very close, and took his hand. He gave her a little squeeze, which she returned. Then she turned and left Adam to his silence, knowing she'd come back and sit in this room another time, and he'd let her.

She wandered across to the other side of the apartment, and looked through the open door of his bedroom but didn't go in. She admired the large framed charcoal drawing above the bed-head, the naked back of a woman, and wondered about the artist.

She then went to another bedroom door, which was just ajar. "Can I sticky-beak?" she asked, realising it would be a guest bedroom.

"Sure, go ahead." Adam was back in the kitchen, watching her move around the apartment. "You're like a little cat, inquisitive about a new space."

"I figured you probably were a cat person," she replied, remembering her thought from the restaurant that Adam and Maddy were like a pair of circling panthers, and she the prey in between. She was still in between them, still curious, but she wasn't afraid.

Juliette pushed the door open and wandered into the room, checking out its neatly made bed and empty wardrobes. Not quite empty. She bent down to pick up a scrap of cloth from the floor of one of the wardrobes, and saw it was a bikini bottom, bright yellow, very brief. She held it to her hips, and thought its owner would have been a similar build as herself. Intrigued, she put it to her nose and breathed it in, to find a sea-salt smell. Whoever wore it, had worn it in the sea. A quick image of dry salty skin flashed into her mind, some psychic connection with a girl in a yellow bikini, a reminder of summer.

She took the little garment out to Adam and waved it under his nose. "Company, Adam? Was she all salty and delicious?"

"Ah, where'd you find that? I got a message from Leslie, saying she'd left it somewhere, could I look. I completely forgot." He turned the bottoms over in his hand, as if he wasn't quite sure what to do with the fragment of cloth.

"On the wardrobe floor. Who's Leslie?"

"Leslie? An American girl, stayed here with a friend for several weeks over summer. The other girl's the niece of a colleague in America. Nice kids, still studying."

"Two young things, Adam? Did you behave?" She caught a look on his face, and laughed. "You didn't behave, did you? You sly dog, Adam, you sly old dog." She looked up at him and pouted. "Now you've just made it difficult for me. You'll want to compare." She stopped teasing for a moment. "Wait. You said girls, kids. How old were these two, dare I ask?"

"Twenty-two-ish, I think," he replied. "Thereabouts."

"You think? That's almost cradle snatching, Adam. Goodness me, you're a bad man. Still, that makes me not so bad, being a bit older than that."

"Not so bad for what, Juliette?"

"Don't be coy, Adam. We both know why I'm here."

They looked at each other, both smiling, and Juliette considered the fact that every time she'd met this man, there'd been sex involved. First the crazy Madelyn in the restaurant toilets, then Adam and Maddy in the garden, then the ropes. Mouths and fingers, fingers in cunts, fingers around his cock. Juliette had seen Maddy give Adam head in the rope room, so she knew they were intimate, too. She'd liked watching them, seeing Adam's slow release, Madelyn's surprising gentleness.

But Juliette knew, without knowing their history, that Maddy and Adam weren't a couple, they weren't together; just as she and Adam were strangers, despite an innate, instinctive trust. Juliette felt she could trust Adam with her life.

She fingered the lace collar around her throat. She wasn't so sure about Madelyn, though. She thought Madelyn might discard those she lost interest in rather quickly. In a sudden flash of insight, Juliette wondered if Maddy had been discarded herself, and was therefore hard, as a defence. She thought of Madelyn's porcelain skin, might it shatter?

Her train of thought was interrupted.

"Why you're here, Juliette? You rang me, remember, so isn't this for you?" Adam gestured around the apartment with his hands. "I've provided the stage, but aren't you providing the script?"

"I suppose so. But I... I sort of wanted to see what happens. In an unscripted kind of a way. I mean, you didn't say, 'Bad idea, Juliette,' did you? To me coming here."

"No, you're right, I didn't. And you're here."

"We're both here, and I'm hungry," said Juliette. "This... philosophising, isn't going to fill my belly, is it?"

He laughed. "A ravenous creature? Come on then, bring some of this through to the balcony. We can put our feet up out there, while it's still warm enough." Adam picked up a tray full of nibbles and moved out to the balcony. Juliette followed with two bottles of wine and some glasses.

"I've gotta say, that's a pretty special view," she said, leaning on the railing, looking out to the west where the sun was lowering red over a flat sea. "Ten floors up, huh? Can see for miles, from up here. It's quiet, too; that's nice, isn't it?"

"Peaceful, yes, but close enough to the city. See, there's the tram."

"And the light on the hills, that's beautiful too. Lucky man, living here. It's very peaceful, really lovely."

Adam came up behind her and placed his arms around her, his hands resting intimately over her belly. Juliette leaned back against his shoulder, placing her hands over his.

"You're very peaceful too, Adam, but I guess you know that. After the ropes, I felt so very, very safe, like a little girl would be, with her daddy." Juliette's voice was low, and she kept looking out at the view as she spoke. "But you took me hard, when I was tied. You didn't hold back."

"Too hard?" Adam asked.

"Not to your edge, so no, not too hard." She still didn't look at him as she shifted her boundaries, moved her line. Juliette wondered exactly where Adam's edge was.

Suddenly, she rushed forward as if to hurl herself over the balcony railing.

"Whoa!" Adam grabbed her, wrapping his arms hard around her, dragging her quickly back. "What are you doing? Fuck, don't do that!"

She turned to him, passion black in her eyes, adrenalin surging in her body. Adam's eyes flared, and he dragged her further back, away from the edge, pulling her away until he fell into one of the lounge chairs. Juliette fell back on top of him, her arms and legs tangled in his. A shoe fell off as she struggled, and she pushed her hip into his groin. She slid up, grinding her thigh against his, and was rewarded with a ridge that was cock, not muscle.

Her breath was fast, so was his. "Jesus," she exclaimed, "that was quick." She reached for the back of Adam's neck, pulling her mouth to his. Her kiss was fierce, hungry, greedy for him. He responded just as hard, fucking her mouth with his tongue, his hands pulling her close to his body, clamping the tight muscles of her ass in his hands, his strength surging over her. Relentlessly, Juliette fought him and found him, forcing her lighter weight down onto his body, her hands everywhere, trying to find how to bind herself to him, to become as one.

Breathless, they broke the fierce kiss and fell away from each other. Juliette saw darkness in his eyes and her whole body shivered, goose bumps on her arms. "Ohhh, yesss," she hissed, and kissed him again, then pushed him away. She pressed her hand to his groin and gripped the swell there. "Fucking yes, 'till it hurts."

"Fuck, Juliette, what's this about?"

"You know, Adam, you fucking know." Juliette sat up, her thighs clamping his, her high breasts rising fast with her breath. "I got you going there, didn't I?"

She placed her hand on his throat, grasping him with her full hand width and squeezing. Juliette looked deep into Adam's eyes, thrilling to the turmoil there, and all the while she kept pressing on his throat. Eventually he gasped and she released him; suddenly her body felt lighter over his.

Juliette eased herself off him, and primly swept her hand back through her hair, tidying herself. She stood up, collected her shoe and put it back on; then sat back in the second lounger chair. "I think I'll have that drink now, Adam. White wine, can I?"

Adam composed himself too, as if nothing had happened. Juliette watched him intently. "Not a kitten, then; the cat?" he asked.

Juliette laughed, a high, sweet laugh. "Still a kitten, Adam. With tiny claws."

"Christ," he replied, "sharp enough."

"Wait till I bite, my sharp little teeth," said Juliette, reaching for some cheese and several crackers. She waved her hand over the landscape. "Nice view, it really is."

She smiled, because Adam was looking at her with lust in his eyes.

Juliette got up, pulled her chair nearer to Adam's, then slipped both shoes off, putting them neatly just inside the door. She sat back down, putting her feet up on the edge of Adam's seat, her knees up high. She pushed the flow of her dress down between her legs so her thighs were hidden. She poked Adam playfully with her toe. "Do you like my feet, Adam? Bonnard says I have delicate little feet, just right for dancing. See." She pointed both feet together, and placed them in his lap.

"Who's Bonnard. You mentioned him in the garden, as well."

"He's Madelyn's dresser, her couturier. He fitted me for lingerie, does all of Maddy's, too."

"Lucky man," said Adam.

"You will be. Don't be hasty."

He laughed. "You sound just like Maddy."

"Do I, darling?" Juliette mimicked the other woman, perfectly.

"Christ," Adam chuckled. "Don't let her hear you say that. She'll have your guts for garters, taking the piss like that."

"So you can unclip her stockings from my stretched out bits around her waist, roll them down those long legs of hers?" Juliette enjoyed teasing Adam and conspiring with him against Maddy. She wouldn't be so brave with Madelyn.

"Well, I haven't got to those long legs yet. Her denial is... thorough and complete."

"Oh Adam, you poor man, it must be so... frustrating." Juliette watched his face carefully as she spoke, and spotted the unconscious flare in his eyes, before he caught himself. *I'm right*, she thought, *it is*. "We'll have to do something about that."

"Tell me about Bonnard," said Adam, changing the subject, and taking Juliette's feet in his hands, giving her a long, slow foot massage.

Interesting, thought Juliette, *he doesn't want to talk about Madelyn. Not yet, anyway.*

She sighed with pleasure from his strong hands on her feet, and told Adam of her encounter with Bonnard. She delighted in the way his cock stirred when she described how she'd stood over Madelyn, then been fucked by her mistress's fingers. *He wants to hear about her, though.*

"Look at the beautiful colours Bonnard found for me," she said, undoing the top buttons of her dress to reveal the lacy top of her bra and the shallow valley of her cleavage. "Blue, just like your eyes."

Juliette did one button up to hide the bra, and took a long, slow sip of wine, all the time looking over the top of the glass and gazing into Adam's eyes. Then, quite deliberately, she winked.

"Fuuck," whispered Adam.

"Adam! You're a bad man. Wait, you naughty boy."

"Jesus, the pair of you, you're both the bloody same."

Juliette grinned, and licked her lips with the tip of her little red tongue.

"You just encourage us, Adam."

"Me? I don't do anything."

"Precisely. But that lets us do exactly what we want. And we want different things, Madelyn and I. But curiously, both from the same man. Can you be that man for both of us, do you think?"

"I seem to be managing okay, so far," replied Adam, his look steady, accepting hers.

"Oh yes, you are. That's why I'm here." Juliette didn't pretend.

"Haven't we had this conversation already?"

"Yes, but that only got us to hors d'oeuvres. Now I want something proper to eat. I'm still hungry."

"There's a little bistro five minutes away. We can go there."

When they went out, Juliette left her keys on the kitchen bench.

"That," said Juliette, leaning back in her chair, "was delicious. I'm so full I can hardly move." She rested her hands on her belly, glad she wasn't wearing tight jeans.

Adam reached forward with a serviette to dab a little bit of cream from her lip, from the dessert.

"You're indulging me, aren't you," she said to Adam. "I like it. I like you. I can see why Maddy does. Should she be jealous?" Juliette was covering all bases, but still manoeuvring around Madelyn.

"I'm not sure Maddy does jealous. I've seen no evidence of it. I'm not sure you'd know, if she did. But she's not here, so speculation's a bit pointless, isn't it?" Adam looked around the little bistro, still busy with its early evening bookings. "Do you want anything else, a coffee?"

"No thanks; fully fed, fully fucked, all's good."

"Getting ahead of yourself, Juliette?" Adam smiled.

"Just ticking them off, so I don't forget in the morning."

"Is this foreplay?" Adam asked.

"Probably," she replied. "Come on, let's go."

Adam looked for the waiter, but Juliette just got up and stood by the till.

As they walked back to Adam's apartment, Juliette tucked her arm in his but didn't say anything. Her three inch heels clicked on the pavement. Bonnard was right, three inches was the perfect height for her delicate frame. She looked up at Adam with a little smile.

"Get undressed please," Juliette asked, three minutes after they'd got inside the door, one minute after Adam had put a CD on, turning the volume down low. "It's playtime."

Juliette watched Adam's reaction, his eyebrow slightly raised, but she'd already primed him during the meal, and she banked on him indulging her more, to see how far she'd go, to see how far he'd follow.

She knew something of her own predilections, having been bound and tied several times before, and skirmished with light and delicate pain. She wondered about Adam, because he'd taken her quite hard the second time, but not hard enough. He'd held himself back; for care of her or fear of himself. Juliette didn't know, so she'd dance around his darkness, lightly.

She watched him undo his shirt buttons, un-notch his belt, bend down to loosen his laces, flick off his shoes. Adam watched Juliette watching him as he took his shirt off and slid his trousers down his legs with simple and efficient movements.

Some men, Juliette knew, would turn away from her gaze, slightly nervous; others might joke a little, or strut. Adam did none of that, he simply stood before her naked. Juliette liked his elegant simplicity, knowing he was comfortable in his own place. It would be nothing unusual for him to be naked in his home.

"I'm over-dressed," she said. "Come here."

Juliette stood in the middle of the lounge room while Adam undid the buttons down the front of her dress, kneeling before her to get at the lowest ones, then standing to take the dress from her shoulders. He neatly folded the garment and placed it over the back of the lounge. The pale cream cotton complemented the darker leather of the furniture.

"Look at that, accessorising. You could make cushions," Juliette said, turning to see.

"I get mine from Ikea," he replied. "I'm too lazy to shop around."

"Damn," she said. "I'm not Swedish."

"You'll do."

She looked at Adam closely, wondering exactly how he got away with saying something like that. "My God," she said, with delight in her voice, "here I am, standing half naked in a room with a fully naked man, and you're saying 'you'll do.' 'You'll do?' Fuck me, that's a cheek. A girl should be affronted, a girl should."

"No different to you saying, 'get undressed, please.' Anyway, it's not like I'm asking you to drive a Volvo." He paused, grinning. "Or a Saab."

Juliette laughed, a high peal of a laugh that was pure delight. "God, you're wonderful. Can I come here more often? 'Or a Saab,' I like that!"

She turned around to present her back and the thin strap of her bra to Adam. "Undo me, funny man."

"With pleasure, my lovely."

On hearing the endearment, Juliette's mood suddenly shifted, and she just wanted to be close to Adam; no sex, just talk, wanting to be held.

She folded the cups of the bra together and placed it on top of the dress. Juliette took his hand and led him through to the spare bedroom.

"Not in your bed, Adam, not till I'm properly invited."

She carefully folded the bed covers down and plumped up the pillows. She turned to him, gazing at him with dark and serious eyes, relying on his intuition to sense her change of mood. "Get in," she said softly, and slid herself alongside his comforting body. Adam held her, just as he'd held her when the ropes came off. Juliette floated in a safe place, his heartbeat in her ear a soothing, steady hush.

"Tell me about your first girl," she asked, "when you were very young."

She snuggled into his chest as Adam told her the story of Pamela, his first girl, in his soft, almost English accent. With a belly full of food and a warm and comfortable bed, Juliette drifted off to sleep, lulled by his voice. Sometimes she needed comfort far more than sex.

An hour or so later, Juliette surfaced from the depths of sleep, vaguely aware of an emptiness beside her, and quiet movement outside the room. The apartment was in darkness, lit only by a faint ambient light from the rising moon, not enough to properly see by. She saw a shape move outside the bedroom door, and heard a door open. A few seconds later she heard the toilet seat go up, followed by the sound of water on water, then silence.

She swung her feet to the floor and got up, conscious of her bladder, realising that it must be Adam taking a piss. She needed one too, so moved carefully through the apartment, guessing her way in the dark.

"Ouch," she exclaimed, not guessing well enough and stubbing her toe on a chair. "I can't see."

"Sorry," she heard Adam's voice, "I didn't want to disturb you. Light switch, just inside the door."

"Thanks. You don't mind?"

"No, it's okay."

Juliette flicked the light on. "God, that's bright." She moved up behind Adam, rested her cheek against his back, and curled a hand around to cover his, to hold him holding his cock as he finished his piss.

"That's intimate, Juliette."

"Why not?" She kissed his back. "Don't flush."

She let go of Adam's hand as he gave his cock a few last shakes, and took in the pungency of his urine, breathing in deeply. She remembered her words to Bonnard, 'Don't forget to smell me.'

Adam turned from her and moved to the sink to wash his hands.

"Wait," Juliette said. "Me, too."

She swiftly pulled her panties down, leaving them on the bathroom floor, then put the seat down and sat, legs parted. "Hold me," she said, taking Adam's hand and holding it under her. Looking up at him with a serious, concentrated look on her face, she sighed and let go her pee, which ran hot over Adam's hand and splashed fountain-like into the bowl. She closed her eyes in relief as she let her piss run long. "I've always wanted to do that," she said.

"Cats marking. You're just like Madelyn."

"When did she do it?"

"On the way to the restaurant that night. Deliberately peed on the ground I was standing on."

"Did you move your feet away?"

"No."

"You don't mind being marked, then?"

"Doesn't look like it, does it?"

Juliette looked up at him, moved his hand away, and wiped herself with toilet paper. In her mind's eye she saw the cream of Madelyn's cunt on her fingers and the stripe of russet red at the base of the woman's pale, alabaster belly, displayed in the toilet cubicle at the restaurant, like a painting on a wall at the end of a long corridor.

She laughed. "I feel like I'm in a Kubrick movie. Sex and death in bathrooms."

Adam turned to the sink and washed his hands. "Something else to talk about over coffee. So many scenes!"

Juliette washed her hands too. "Tiles would be too cold on my bum, though. And a hard floor, that's not me."

"Done that already. Had to cook at four in the morning, too. You keep sensible hours, Juliette."

Juliette turned the bathroom light off, and led Adam back to the spare bedroom, pulling him along with her hand on his cock, which was thickening under her grip.

"Plenty of time, then," she said, "with my sensible hours."

"For what?" he asked.

"Me."

"Juliette's playtime, played out in sensible time?"

"Exactly like that. *Quid pro quo,* Adam, if you're game."

She looked at him, judging whether he grasped her meaning without prompting. A further thickening of his cock hinted that Adam was willing to go somewhere at her bidding, or at least, the instinctive creature inside him was. Juliette sat on the end of the bed, holding his cock in both hands, watching as his shaft straightened in front of her eyes.

"It's fascinating to watch," she said, "how a man's prick does that, grow by itself. Tell me what you're thinking, Adam, what's turning you on, just thinking it?"

She looked up into his eyes, waiting for his response.

"No one thing, and everything. A naked woman, leading me by the cock. Undressing you, your lace of blue. The heat of your piss on my hand. Your intimacy, doing that. Your confidence, Juliette. That cracked edge in your voice when you know exactly what you're asking for."

Adam pulled her up from the bed so she stood before him, his hands on her waist. "You're like some wild animal, but if I wanted to tame you I couldn't. I wouldn't want to, either."

"I'm that little inquisitive cat of yours, with its tiny sharp claws." Juliette pinched up Adam's nipples with both hands, her nails pulling up the points of flesh to tight peaks. Adam shivered with the sharp pleasure, and Juliette felt his cock pulse against her belly.

"And its little sharp teeth," she added, before biting a nipple lightly with her teeth, then sucking the whole nipple to bring up the blood, and biting again.

She leaned into him, making him spread his feet on the floor to keep balance. Juliette turned herself slowly, steering Adam's body so he faced away from the bed. Then she leaned against him once more, and even though she was a good head shorter than he was, she had an insistent strength that pushed him back until his legs touched the edge of the bed. Juliette took a step back, placed one hand on his chest and pushed, quickly, hard. Adam fell backwards onto the bed.

She stood over him, with her hands on her hips, a look of delight in her eyes.

"It's all about balance, and knowing when to push," she explained. "Move up the bed; but then, don't move any more, not without me saying." As she spoke, Juliette lowered her voice, an old actor's trick to command attention. She saw the depths of his eyes deepen, his pupils dilating as Adam shifted up a sensory notch. His fingers gripped the sheet, once, twice, like a spasm.

Juliette stepped up onto the bed and stood over Adam, her feet on each side of his hips. "Look at me slowly, Adam. I want to feel my skin burn, where you see me."

She stood over him and watched his eyes drop, looking down to her legs, her calves. Like Bonnard he took in every curve, and the linger of his look was like Maddy's slow hands turned to ghosts. Juliette shivered; to be craved for by these people made her hungrier.

Juliette watched the movement of Adam's slow eyes up her legs, and saw his gaze stop when it reached her centre, her sex. She lowered her body just the tiniest bit, enough to tighten the muscles of her thighs, to quiver tension into her limbs. She moved her hands to the bottom of her belly and held them motionless there. She saw Adam's cock throb in anticipation, waiting for her next movement.

She slid fingers to her sex and spread her lips, showing Adam her glistening colours.

"Fuuck, just like Madelyn does," he whispered.

Juliette's eyes went dark and wide at the sound of the other woman's name. Adam had invoked Madelyn into the room, but Juliette would harness the added energy for herself.

"Madelyn's a finger fuck slut, Adam, three fingers fucked. I don't know if she even likes cock." Juliette made the other woman sound crude, and saw his cock throb, again.

She suddenly dropped down to her knees, gripping Adam's hips between her thighs. She leaned forward, her breasts dropping and brushing against his chest, and nuzzled up until her hot breath sighed in his ear. "I'll fuck you first, Adam, that's a promise. Not Madelyn; me, Juliette."

Juliette knew that names were powerful things, and by having both spoken, she could fuck with his mind before he fucked her. " I'll. Fuck. You. First." She reinforced it, to keep him off balance.

Adam opened his mouth to speak.

Juliette put a finger to his lips. "Ssshh, no need. I'll look after you, Adam, you'll see."

She stretched his arms up above his head, her dropping breasts sliding over his face. "Don't move. Think of Maddy, think of me." Juliette led him down his own path, just like she did in the Japanese garden.

She got off the bed, leaned over and took Adam's cock in her hand, and kissed it once, in the centre of the shaft. "Your cock, Adam, is very, very beautiful. You can have it back when I'm finished. Don't move. Back in a sec."

She went out to her bag and found the four long silk scarves, a soft leather collar and the long and delicate chain she'd put there when she'd left her house earlier that evening.

She'd gone back to Bonnard alone to explain what she wanted, and he'd boxed the things up beautifully for her. "Juliette, my darling girl," he'd said, his eyes bright with affection for her, "you really are astonishing." He'd kissed her cheek. "Don't hurt him."

"Only when I stop," she'd replied.

"Adam," she said, returning to the room and showing him the scarves, "do you want me like this?"

Adam looked back at Juliette, his cock thick and hard, angled up from his gut. He separated his legs a few inches, showing her the dark mass of his balls.

"Oh," she said, smiling, "I see. No words then? None needed."

She swiftly tied one of the scarves around an ankle, splaying his leg wide, then crouched on the floor to knot the other end around the leg of the bed. She repeated the action on Adam's other leg. "I'm not Roshi-san, but these knots will do."

She crawled up Adam's body to sit on his chest. "Arms, over your head, or stretched out wide?"

Adam moved his wrists together, his arms held above his head.

"Fair enough," she said, lowering her sex to his face as she tied his wrists together. She stretched her arms out, holding his bound hands to the bed, and eased herself back onto his mouth. She stayed there, enjoying his attention, until she could smell her own aroma rising.

"Peaches and cream, Adam, and Maddy with strawberries in her luscious cunt?"

Juliette was content to have two women in the room for Adam, because she knew he only had one tongue, and it was in her.

"I've changed my mind. You wanted your wrists together, so I'll tie them apart, spread-eagled."

Juliette lifted her sex away from Adam's mouth, and held herself six inches above his eyes so he could see her sex but not reach it. She quickly undid the bonds on his wrists, then dropped down for his mouth on her hole. She pushed herself back for a single probe of his tongue, so he had the taste of her ass. She then rolled away to one side of the bed, where she stretched out his arm and tied it up by the bed head, looping the scarf quickly down around the leg of the bed.

"Hmmm, I don't know. Adam, should I leave your other hand free, so you can grab my flesh, or tie you all up so you can't?" She looked down on him, knowing he wouldn't even hint, for she'd do the other thing, to deny him. "Can't you decide?" she teased.

Juliette got back onto the bed and sat with her heels tucked under her bottom, and studied her captive man. As she did so, she gently took his cock and began to slowly play with it, her hand gliding in slow looping movements up and down his shaft, up over the plum dark head, gliding, gliding.

Adam's eyes closed as he sank into her care, and gave himself over to his pleasure. She watched his face, and felt peaceful herself, stroking, stroking, her breathing slowing to the rhythm of her hand. She did this for some minutes, arousing him slowly, watching his response, his faster breathing. She shifted to the other side of the bed and, as she knew he would, his untied hand touched her skin gently, feeling her softness, caressing her curves. This was a mood she liked, a slow beginning with a lover, everything focussed on where the touch was, nothing more.

Juliette rolled off the bed and kneeled beside it. She placed her cheek in the palm of his untied hand and, as she knew he would, he held her without moving, his hand a little pillow. She kissed his palm and the soft skin of his wrist, just a gentle touch of her lips, and then wrapped the last scarf around it with a silken knot, and tied him to the bed.

Juliette stood beside the bed, looking down on the spread-eagled Adam tied for her pleasure, her slow tease. She wondered what to do first.

She picked up the delicate chain, and looped it three times around her waist and clipped the ends together, admiring the way it clung to her hips.

"It's very delicate, isn't it?" She put a finger to her lips to silence his reply. She then placed the fine leather choker on his belly where his cock could lie upon it, if he lost his blood hard erection. She smiled, as Adam's cock angled up away from his gut. She watched, fascinated, seeing a pulse beat in a big vein that curved along the shaft and disappeared into the shadow where his balls were tight, high up in his groin. Juliette's eyes darkened with growing lust for this cock inside her, and she wondered how long she could wait.

To give herself some time, she went out to the lounge room and found a CD she knew, which would set a fifty minute cycle, a soundtrack. She grinned, and placed another album nearby, knowing she'd want longer. She went to the fridge to find water, and her eyes fell on the bikini bottom, left on the bench by Adam after she'd found it. On a whim, she slipped it on and pulled it up, adjusting its ties and the little cotton gusset covering her pussy lips.

"Hello Leslie," she whispered, "do you want to be in Adam's head once more? I don't mind." She pictured another girl's sex, and would cup it in her hand and kiss her.

She returned to the bedroom. "Yellow suits me, don't you think?" She pirouetted on her toes to show him.

"Ahh, sweet god, how many women are you going to find?" Adam replied, his voice low; but his cock bounced, again.

"You should tidy up behind you, then, if you don't want me to find them." Juliette crawled up onto the bed, and sat with her cloth covered sex on his shaft. She turned the collar over in her hands, then decided this other girl could be here for now, but she'd have to go before she claimed Adam for the rest of the night. Juliette placed the collar on the bedside table, next to the lamp.

"Did Leslie have a pretty pussy, Adam, with smooth and tidy lips like mine?" Juliette's voice was conversational, she wanted him to picture his Leslie all over again and see two pretty girls in his mind. "Or was she darker there, her lips like petals on a bruised and beautiful flower?" She'd paint him a picture, so much luscious fruit to choose from.

"Did you fuck this girl, Adam, with your lovely long cock, did she squeal?" As she spoke to him, she began to sway back and forth along his shaft, the fabric of the material pulling along her lips, dragging against her clit. She ground down onto him, finding her own pleasure.

"Were her breasts like mine, tight and high? Or did she have bigger boobs that dropped all heavy in your hands? Did she bounce in her little yellow 'kini top when she ran on a long, sandy beach?"

She stopped moving, and her voice turned lascivious. "Or was she like Madelyn, her tits hardly there at all?" She felt a pulse between her legs, and saw Adam lick his lips. "Ohh, Adam. Miss Maddy's got her hooks in you. Fuuck, you want her, don't you, so bad?"

Juliette got up from his body, and peeled the bikini bottoms down her legs. She threw the scrap of cloth out the door. "Bye bye, Leslie," she said, "Adam doesn't want you anymore.

"He doesn't really want me, either, but that's too bad."

Suddenly, as quickly as she'd thrown herself towards the balcony railing, she slapped Adam hard on his cheek, the sound of skin on skin loud in the room. Her fingers burned with a sudden heat. She'd slapped him hard, his cheek would sting.

Adam's eyes flashed open black as ink. He instinctively pulled up against the scarves but they held him back. "What the fuck?" he exclaimed.

"I've decided, Adam, that I don't want Maddy in the room. I thought I didn't mind, but I do. This obsession you have for her. There's no place for me when she's here."

Juliette ran her fingers lightly over his cheek where she'd slapped him, gauging his reaction. She watched him closely, reading every tiny movement, every sign. She studied his eyes, the way they held hers then slid away, then came back. She stroked the blaze of heat on his cheek and, yes, there it was, that subtle, subtle pressure. Did he even know that he did it, seeking the comfort of her hand even after the sting?

She slapped him again, to find out.

Adam winced, and her hand stung. Juliette looked at her fingers and they were red. She'd slapped him hard, but her heart wasn't in it, not any more.

"This is all a bit fake, isn't it? Play acting. It's an idea of you, all tied up with me in control, but I'm not, am I? In control." She sat beside him on the bed, looking down at Adam's body, the blaze of red on his cheek. "You're just letting me do this, but you're not actually giving anything away, are you? You're not giving yourself up to me. Not really."

Juliette saw him formulating a reply, saw his eyes deepen and draw her down, draw her into a zone of comprehension. "But you don't actually need to say anything, do you? You just let me figure it out for myself. Little Juliette with her silly ideas."

"Not silly, Juliette. Capricious, wilful, passionate, lots of things." He smiled up at her. "But never, ever, silly. You're too clever for that. I don't do 'silly,' Juliette. I don't waste my time."

"But you let me do this."

"Because you wanted to do it; but that doesn't make it silly."

"What is it, then?" Juliette asked.

"A game in a safe place," Adam replied.

"What if I don't want it to be safe?"

"Untie me then, don't play games."

Juliette was silent for a long moment, for a very long moment.

"Would you hurt me?" she finally asked.

"Do you want to be hurt?"

"Yes," Juliette replied simply, her whole purpose with Adam spiralling down to this essential thing, this central desire.

"Untie me, then," Adam said.

"Fuuck," whispered Juliette. "Am I fucking crazy? I don't know you from - "

"Adam. You don't know me from Adam. Yet you came here of your own accord, you tie me up, you play your game, but you want more. You want me to take you some place deeper, darker. Why me, Juliette?"

"Because..." Juliette struggled to articulate why. "Because... you're so fucking kind. Just..." Clarity struck her. "Because you wouldn't hurt me. You might whip me, bruise me, if I wanted it, but in here," and she tapped her temple with a finger three quick times, "you wouldn't hurt me. Not in my head. You couldn't do that. The love that's always in you, it would stop you, every time."

Juliette moved closer to Adam so she sat beside him, his body sprawled naked for her eyes to see, but her eyes were closed so she didn't see. What she didn't see was Adam's stillness, that quiet place in his eyes as he gazed at her, that place where he wouldn't hurt her. "I'd be safe, with you. That's why."

"Untie me, Juliette. You don't need to fight me to have me." He was silent for a long moment. "It's not a war, nobody loses."

"But you lost someone, didn't you Adam? Someone who never came back?" Juliette's intuition was running strong.

"Yes, I did," he said, simply. "But she's not you, Juliette. She's gone. You're here."

She leaned over to unknot the scarf from his wrist then stretched over him to undo the other one, then slid to the bottom of the bed to release his ankles. As she crawled back up to him, she pulled a blanket up with her, to keep them warm. Before she lay her head down on his shoulder, she reached behind her neck to unclip the choker from her throat and placed it within the leather one on the bedside table.

"Can we make love now, Adam? Just you and me, nobody else, no ghosts?"

Juliette was wet, her emotions and passion driven hard and high by their words; her long foreplay, which began in Bonnard's shop, complete. The ebb and flow of the evening, the long sunset and the walk in the dark, Adam's blue eyes that did indeed match her lingerie, all of it came down to this:

Juliette knelt above Adam, her wet sex poised above him, and she took his cock in her hand, placing its head between her lips. She slid it back and forth twice to slick the head with her moisture, then eased down an inch, taking him into her. She stopped, settling herself onto Adam's shaft, easing herself open for him. Juliette placed both hands on his chest, and eased herself down those long inches till he filled her, her clit pressing down onto the root of his cock.

"Oh sweet, sweet fuck, that's..." *beyond words*, she thought, as she held herself still, then collapsed onto Adam's chest, her breasts pressed against his flesh. "Oohh, fuck me slowly, slowly, I can't..." *bear it if you don't move inside me,* "take me, fuck me, love me, Adam; sooo..." softly.

Adam moved gently beneath her, and his hands came up and held her head and brought her mouth to his. They kissed, and it was gentle and sweet; and with two of her fingers Juliette stroked the side of Adam's throat. The skin there was soft and she didn't think a man's skin could be so soft, but it was.

He held Juliette in his arms and made quiet, slow love with her till she melted and could hardly breath and she'd never felt like this before, but oh my god it felt good, so sweet, so warm, and behind her breasts she felt a tight ache and her nipples were rigid, hard, and connected straight to her clit.

Ahh, sweet goodness, Adam was moving faster and Juliette clenched him and gripped him and slid up and slid down hard onto his cock, and they were fucking now, their fingers laced through each other's and Adam's breath was in Juliette's mouth, circling his energy within her. Juliette cried out, moaning with her rising pleasure, closer, closer, her ecstasy climbing, crying out, "Oh god, I'm going to..." and she lost all coherence and went beyond words as Adam fucked her tight cunt so hard, so hard, and Juliette came with a sudden cry, "Ahh, now, fuck yes," and she trembled and shuddered and Adam held her firmly in his arms in the tightest embrace...

... and Juliette came again, and was no weight at all as she lay upon him and slowly caught her breath, kissing him, kissing him. "Just hold me," she sighed, and he did, still hard inside her, not moving.

Slowly Juliette came to her senses and she clenched Adam's cock tightly. "You've not come yet," she said in wonder. "Was that just for me?"

"Ahh, my lovely, my pleasure too, believe me." He hugged her. "Ladies before gentlemen, I've always said," with a lightness in his voice.

Juliette lifted herself off his chest to study him, her elbows on the bed. "I don't think I've ever had a gentleman before, if that's the case."

She clenched herself around his shaft again, and began to move on him.

"Wait," Adam said. "Not here. Come to my bed, Juliette."

She stopped moving, slowly digesting what Adam had just said. *His bed.*

"But..."

"Ssshh, Juliette. Do as you're told." He held her face in his hands. "For once in your life."

Adam turned Juliette on to her side so he could slowly withdraw from her, "Ohh, don't go..." then he rolled from the bed and stood. He picked Juliette up in his arms and carried her from the spare room, her arms held tight around his neck, her eyes wide open, gazing at his face.

Adam carried Juliette through to his bedroom and to his bed. With one hand he pulled back the covers, then placed her gently on the cool sheets. Without fuss, for Juliette was very, very wet, he lay between her legs and placed the head of his cock between her lips, and with one long, sensuous thrust, filled her completely. "Here, my lovely, in my bed, take me."

This time, Juliette held Adam's cheeks in her hands and looked up at him in wonder. "Does this mean," she asked quietly, "I can stay till morning?"

"It does," he replied.

"I'd like that," she said, "very much." She caressed his cheek where she'd slapped him. "In your bed."

Adam made long, gentle love with Juliette; and before he came with a long, moaning sigh deep inside her, she came again, twice. She wondered what he was doing to her because it didn't hurt at all, but she came again, twice.

Late the next morning, after a long, leisurely breakfast which followed a long, leisurely love-making when they first awoke, the eastern light warming the bed, Juliette dressed. She walked quietly around the apartment in her blue lingerie, put on her dress which had been neatly folded on the back of the lounge, and found her shoes by the balcony door. Adam watched her, this confident little cat. She smiled at him, watching her.

Juliette picked up the yellow bikini bottom from the floor where she'd thrown it, and said she'd wash it for him the next time she did her knickers; and he could send it back to Leslie with a hand-written note that said, I found them; and the note needn't mention Juliette at all.

She picked up her car keys from the bench, and made sure her phone and purse were in her bag.

"Can I have a key, do you think?" she asked Adam, and her voice had a slight crack when she said it.

"You'll need to bring Leslie's bikini back, won't you? I'll give it to you then. Next time."

It was only when she got downstairs to her car that Juliette touched her throat and realised Maddy's choker was still on the bedside table, where she'd put it. That was okay; Adam would find it and put it in a beautiful box and she could pick it up next time she saw him. She pondered what she might say to Maddy, but didn't worry too much about that.

She was, after all, a brave little cat and not afraid of big ones. Juliette smiled, and started her car's engine. It was Saturday, and her shift at the restaurant started soon. It was a beautiful day for a drive.

In Madelyn's House

"How was Juliette on the weekend? She told me she saw you." Madelyn took a long slurp from the straw of her chocolate milkshake, swirling the last of it around the bottom of the glass.

"Such class, Madelyn. Can take you to all the best places," remarked Adam, leaning over to wipe a chocolaty dribble from her chin. "Did she tell you she stayed the night? My invitation, of course. Well, sort of. She invited herself for the evening; I said she could stay for the morning."

"Stay the night? She did tell me that. Was she delectable?" Maddy asked.

"You know she is. Peaches and honey in the evening, pancakes in the morning. She liked my cooking."

Maddy laughed. "She liked more than that, lucky girl. When do I get to enjoy your cooking, Mister Cain?" She looked at Adam with her clear, steady gaze.

"When you're hungry, I guess. Whenever that might be." Adam looked right back at her, with a lazy smile. "You'll have to call me. I don't have your number, remember?"

"You're right, you don't. How remiss of me." Maddy ran one red fingernail down the back of Adam's hand and along the length of his middle finger, and thought of his cock in her mouth the night of Juliette's ropes. She wondered what he would feel like inside her, but like a fine wine in a cellar, she could wait.

To give herself a tiny pleasure, a frisson of anticipation, Madelyn ran her finger up the centre of her blouse, bumping over the buttons, while Adam followed the movement with his eyes. She ran her fingers up to the side of her neck, then slid them down inside the blouse and caressed a bare nipple until it tightened. Satisfied with the nerve connecting to her clitoris with a throb, she withdrew her fingers from the shadows of the cloth and touched them to Adam's lips for a kiss.

"Come on," she said, "let's go and see the big cats."

She stood up from the cafeteria table and looped her arm in Adam's. Together they walked down the path to where the lions roamed loose in their enclosure. It was a perfect day to visit the zoo, and the magnificent animals walked with a languid beauty.

Later that evening, after a long and leisurely meal, Maddy and Adam ended up in an intimate basement club with a smooth jazz quintet and a singer with smoke in her voice.

Maddy watched Adam watching the band, and found another place he lost himself in. "Yeah, that's fine, that's good," he murmured, as the drummer cracked a rim-shot and could have cracked a whip, the snap was so crisp and tight.

She lay her arm along the back of the lounge they were sitting on and slowly caressed Adam's neck, just to touch him. Pulled away from the band for a moment, he looked at her, gave her a gentle smile, and touched two fingers to her lips for a kiss.

"You're doing it, Mister Cain," she said, after his fingers left her lips.

"Doing what, Madelyn?"

"Making me want you."

"What would you say if I said you can't have me?" Adam asked.

"I'd say you were a liar, Mister Cain," she replied. "I'm Madelyn, who drives a fast car, remember."

"Where's Maddy, who flirts with men at crossings?"

"Do you know, Mister Cain, I'm not sure." She removed her fingers from his neck and placed her hands in her lap. They weren't trembling, but she wasn't her usual self.

Adam moved closer to her and placed his own fingers on her throat, and caressed it as slowly as she had caressed his. "What are you frightened of, Madelyn?"

"Of giving in. You were meant to want me, endlessly." She looked at him and her eyes softened. "Not the other way round."

"Ohh, Maddy, silly girl. You're not giving up, surely not?"

"You don't do 'silly,' remember. Juliette told me," she replied.

"Just checking, Madelyn." He stroked her cheek, and if she was a cat she'd have purred. "Since you've given in, your place, or mine?"

"That's very forward, Mister Cain." Her eyes brightened as their game began.

"Someone has to be. It's nearly midnight, and there's no pumpkin for a coach."

"No glass slipper either, and I don't think I can run." Madelyn got to her feet, her legs long in a tight pair of designer jeans that left no illusions. She had no illusions either. She'd given in to her base desires and could no longer wait for this man. But she had him where she wanted, coming willingly. She smiled. Just like Juliette, she thought, he's got a mind of his own. She liked that in the girl, and she liked that in the man. It meant she didn't have to do all the thinking.

As she walked in front of the band, Maddy swayed in time to the beat, slow and wicked. "Dance with me, Adam," she said, on a whim, turning to the tiny dance floor.

The drummer noticed and greeted them with a cymbal splash, subtly picking up the beat. The band fell into the pocket and they danced for a while. A small patter of applause saw them off the floor. "Damn, they're good," Adam murmured in her ear. "So are you."

"Perfection, Mister Cain, don't you think?" She leaned against him, her tall, elegant body melding beautifully with his. The drummer momentarily missed a beat, but caught it, just in time.

"Worth the wait, Madelyn, worth the wait."

"Like that fine wine, you naughty boy?"

"I hope so," he replied.

"Is this foreplay, Mister Cain?"

"Probably."

She laughed. She'd been wet for hours, and was way, way past four.

Madelyn drove her car down the long avenue of jacaranda trees shining silvery blue under the high, bright moon. She pulled into the drive of a house hidden from the street by high hedges and a security gate, which slowly opened on command from the remote in the centre console. She eased through the gate and parked the car at the end of a long drive, its wheels crunching on gravel.

Adam stepped from his side of the car, and quickly went around to the driver's side, opening the door for Maddy. She slid her long legs from the car and took his hand. "Welcome to my lair, Mister Cain."

"Will I get out alive?" He looked around, but the grounds were dark and shadowed.

"My gardener does say the graves make mowing difficult," she replied, with a smile.

"You should dig the holes deeper then, Maddy. Or burn the corpses first."

"You make me sound like a monster, Mister Cain." Maddy put the key in the front door, and pushed it open. It was completely silent on its well-oiled hinges. "I'm an angel, really, I assure you."

Adam touched her high on her shoulders as if to find wings, and ushered Maddy into her house.

"Monsieur," she said, "you may hang your hat and cloak on these hooks," pointing to a row of hooks at eye height. A single parasol hung there, waiting for a high sun and a long promenade.

"Madame," he replied, "I don't have a hat and a cloak."

"I know, but if you did, this is where they'd go."

"Madelyn, this house really is very beautiful. Show it to me." He looked at her directly. "Show me where you live."

"Take your shoes off here. Bare feet on timber floors and carpets, feels lovely. Keeps me grounded." She bent from the waist to slip her heels off, and her jeans stretched taut over her ass, for his eyes.

"It's those angel's wings, Maddy. You shouldn't flutter so much." Adam leaned against a wall for balance, and crooked a leg to get at his laces, pulling them loose and slipping the shoe off his foot. He repeated

114

the action, and put his shoes and socks under a small rack by the door. He looked up to see her smiling down at him.

"Kiss me here, by the door. A kiss for each room, don't you think?" Maddy stepped forward, undid two buttons on his shirt, and placed her hand behind his neck. She waited. Adam did the same, flicking two buttons from under her throat. The dance that started in the club continued.

"Is it a big house, Madelyn?" he asked.

"Come with me and find out." She pulled him to her.

Their first kiss in the hall was slow, exploratory. Neither of them rushed, they didn't need to. Maddy knew Adam's patience by now, knew it well, and the slow seduction calmed her, but at the same time, inflamed her. Time slowed, and they went into a dream.

Their second kiss, in the front lounge, was longer. The room had a fireplace opposite the door.

"This is one of my favourite places on cold winter nights, a proper log fire, toasted crumpets and marshmallows on a stick."

A deep bay window looked out over a statue of Diana in the middle of the front lawn. Total privacy was assured by the high hedges. Madelyn pulled the drapes wide open and let the moonlight pour in. "It's lovely when it rains."

Adam undid more buttons on Maddy's blouse and pulled the cloth up from the waist of her jeans. His fingers slid inside the garment and circled shivers up and down her spine. She did the same with his shirt, pressing her bare breasts to his naked chest. They slid onto a couch inside the bay window. Adam removed her top and suckled his lips to a hard nipple. Maddy held his head there and wondered if he could feel her heart beat. She could feel it, and didn't want it to slow, not yet.

"I can imagine it, the rain falling on the ground," he replied. She'd forgotten about the rain, in that short moment.

She lay there, his mouth on her tit, and felt curiously, astonishingly, maternal. Is this what it's like to suckle a child? she thought, but it wasn't, as Adam transferred his attention to her other breast and tugged its nipple thick and tight and nearly painful between his lips. This is a man at my breast, not a boy. He moved his mouth away, lower down her belly to the delicate whorl of her navel, which he fucked with his tongue, like a tiny little cunt. But she remained fascinated by her breasts, as if she'd never seen them before.

They had become almost entirely nipple from his strong suck. Usually, her nipples were a delicate shade of pink, floating on her small, pale breasts like cherry blossoms on snow, but his suck had engorged them till they were long and hard, and the hot blood made them redder, thick and dark. Maddy looked down at her breasts, her thick nipples, and pressed her palms against them. She squeezed and rotated her hands, and a wave of hot pleasure spread through her chest, jabbing down to her clitoris. She juddered on the edge of orgasm, imagining her clit engorged and thick, the same rich red.

Maddy moaned, wrapping her long legs around his body, trapping him against her. "You're not going anywhere, Adam."

"I'm not escaping you, Maddy, I'm trying to get inside." He eased back up her torso, and once again found her mouth with his.

Maddy found his hands and pulled them up above her head, stretching herself out, giving herself up to his weight. "Take your time, "she said. "This slow attention is delirious. I want you to feast on me all night."

"Loving you slowly, isn't that a line from a song?" Adam asked.

"Killing me softly."

"Same thing." Adam kissed her again.

"Jesus, where did I find you?" she sighed, "loving me, killing me, same thing... sweet god, kill me some more..."

"In the street. You found me in the street. You said, 'don't push the button,' but it was too late." Adam touched her cheek. "I'd pressed it. That's where I was, and you found me." He winked at her. "The tight skirt helped, and the red sole shoes."

She waited, knowing he'd say something more.

"Your fingers in your cunt, they helped, too." He grinned, and was so lazy with it.

116

Her eyes sparkled with joy. "Ahh, I wondered if you'd noticed. You went very quiet."

"You were rather splendid, Madelyn. I think we talked about perfection."

"We did. Have we found it, do you think?"

"Not yet. Take me to another room, we might find it there."

"Why, do you want to be perfectly wicked, Adam?"

"Not yet."

"Promises, my delightful man?" Maddy got up from the couch, her naked torso glowing under the moonlight and her darkened nipples still jutting hard and long. "Come on then, let's see what else we've got." She took Adam by the hand, and went back to the central hall. "There's the dining room," she said, "but we've eaten, so that's a waste, don't you think?

"And the kitchen, there's the island bench and the cook-top, it's the latest thing." Maddy presented it all as if she was a magnificently decadent real-estate agent, perfectly accustomed to meeting potential buyers in the nude, the sweeping movements of her slender arms drawing Adam's eyes constantly to her body, nowhere else.

"And look, here's a little sewing room, where ladies can retire." Maddy flicked a light switch on and dimmed the lights right down. It might have been a sewing room once, but now it was a comfortable den. A day bed was placed in a corner, under a window curtained against the night. Several books were haphazardly placed on side tables, and a cat lay curled on a chair. It was a lived-in kind of a room, where Maddy found a quiet place. What better place, she thought, for a quiet man with darkness in his eyes to find me.

"Undo me, Adam. In your slow, special way, just undo me.

"Don't tease me, not anymore." Her mood shifted, and she was tired of herself, tired of waiting. "Just fuck me. You can love me in the morning. Fuck me slow and fuck me deep, just don't let it stop." She looked at him with smouldering eyes. "Can you do that, Adam?"

Because Madelyn was who she was, even when giving herself up, she challenged this man to take her. She'd see if he could, by morning.

Adam started with himself, letting Madelyn see what she did to him. He led her to the bed, and she lay upon it, propped on the pillows, watching him. He took three steps back, and undid the belt and fly of his pants. In one fluid, efficient motion he bent and slid the pants down his legs, pulling them off his feet. He stood, and his long cock reached high to the base of his navel, already rigid for her. She liked his showmanship, it seemed natural for a man with a fine cock not to hide it.

She licked her lips, remembering the taste of his flesh, his cum in her mouth when she took him. Maddy kept her eyes on his shaft as Adam moved towards her, wanting this cock to impale her. Still showing himself off, he bent over to undo the belt and buttons of her jeans, his erection proud before her eyes. She could touch him if she wanted to, but like Adam when he first saw her cunt, she just looked.

She inhaled, and could smell his hot maleness. She licked her lips again, to hold that scent on her tongue. He was so close to her.

"Say my name, so I can hear it," Maddy whispered.

"Madelyn Jane, who wants to be fucked."

She shook her head, no. Yes.

"Maddy, then, to love me in the morning?"

Yes. No.

"How do you know, who is who?" She looked up at him, "Which is which?"

"I don't. Neither do you. Does it matter?" Adam pulled her tight jeans down those long legs to reveal pale thighs and her alabaster belly, her sex hidden from his eyes by a tiny patch of cloth. A little blaze of russet red hair was neat above the cloth, at the base of her belly.

"Spread your legs, Madelyn. Show me." Maddy slid her legs wide apart, obedient to him, giving in. She wanted to be fucked, and wanted it his way, to be in his hands. She could fight him later, when she needed herself back and could taunt him.

"Touch yourself, Madelyn." She did as she was told.

"Take it off, smell yourself." She peeled the g-string down her legs, bending up her knees to do so. She held the cloth, saturated with her honey juices, to her nose, breathing herself in. "Rub it over your face, your breasts. Scent yourself, Madelyn, like a cat."

She did as she was commanded, inhaling her scent deeply, marking her face and breasts with her wetness from the tiny piece of cloth.

"Taste me too, Adam, lick my skin. I want -"

"Sshhh, Madelyn. It's what I want, not you." Adam looked down at her, and Madelyn closed her eyes to stop his gaze. She didn't see his gentle smile but she heard it in his voice. "I'll take care of you, Maddy."

In one final act of desire before she was taken, Madelyn rolled over and knelt before Adam, her beautiful cunt slit and the dark pink star of her other hole presented high for his eyes, his cock, his tongue, his finger and his fuck. She rested her weight on her elbows, her hands pushing back against the wall, ready for him to enter her, hard. She sighed, a long wrenching sigh which emptied her lungs completely. He'd make her breathe deeply and fill her, she had no doubt about that, no doubt at all.

"Fuck, that's perfection," murmured Adam.

Madelyn smiled into her pillows, revelling in the awe she inspired. She'd be fucked now by a man who had been waiting a long time, tormented by her magnificent body and her fascinating mind. She thought she and Adam would be a rather good match; they were so very much like each other. Two peas in a pod, she thought, a man with a mirror. She thought he might take vengeance, being made to wait so long, and Madelyn thought she might like that too, very much.

"Fucked like an animal, then, is that how you want it?" He'd read her mind.

"Ohh yes," she crooned, "like a beast in rut."

Adam climbed on the bed behind her and spread her wider, his knees against the inside of hers. He ran his fingers slowly up the insides of her thighs, making her tremble as he found those sensitive places. But he avoided the hollows of flesh near her sex, and ran his hands over the taut, quivering muscles of her ass. He pulled her cheeks even wider apart, and brought his head down closer to blow hot breath over the pucker of her asshole. Maddy jolted at the hot sensation, and she gripped the pillows tightly.

"Yesss," she hissed, "more. Yes, more..."

Adam denied her by taking his breath away, but he continued the slow caress of her ass, her haunches, the long ribbed sides of her torso. He leaned his chest against her back, and the fierce heat of his cock pressed up against her sex, sliding deliriously over her lips. He pushed his shaft against her, then pulled away, slick and wet. He leaned forward again, to take the tight drop of her tits in his hands, squeezing hard, gripping the hard flesh up against her chest.

"Ooo, yeeess, hold me, hold me, oh fuck, just hold me."

He held Madelyn tight in his arms, squeezing her breasts again, pulling her body up against his. And then let her go, his tight wrap gone, leaving her body to shake and shudder alone. He did it all over again, only this time, instead of his breath against her anus, he covered that place completely with his hot mouth, sucking her up, opening his mouth wide to take her flesh in. Maddy pushed herself up and onto his mouth, wanting more.

"Mmmm, fuu uck. Eat me, get inside me. Ooo, ye... ess." She shuddered, and thrust herself back, forcing her ass onto Adam's mouth. But he was gone.

Then he came back, and this time ate her cunt. And again, gone. Then back, biting the flesh of her ass cheeks. Gone, and for three minutes Adam made her wait, before he touched her again. Then gone.

Madelyn moaned and shuddered, cried out, wanting more, wanting him, but still Adam teased and taunted her, his hands and mouth on her; his hands and mouth, gone. His hot, hard shaft burning against her back. Then gone. Her scent rose in the room, mingling with Adam's musk, then the smell of his cock, gone away. He started to taunt her, using her name, talking to her, and all the time it was his hands and his mouth, and the heat of his cock, but never its length inside her.

She didn't know how Adam did it, how he could deny himself her cunt. Madelyn knew she was swollen, fecund and hot. She could feel her own heat radiate, she smelt her hot scent, her own thick odour, her raw animal smell. She could smell her own wet juice, and the room filled with their hot sweat, his dark pheromonal smell, her metallic blood odour, her heat. She ached for his fill, his thickness, his length, wanting to be all fucked up inside, to her depths, fucked full. But he denied her. He wouldn't do it, he held his cock back, his juice, his cum, he wouldn't fuck her.

He wouldn't, he didn't. Madelyn was denied her ultimate fill. Adam teased her, tormented her mind, her flesh, but still he made her wait. And deep down inside, Madelyn triumphed, for in denying her he denied himself too. She felt his want, she heard his ragged breath, she felt his hands begin to tremble.

She began to speak, to taunt him, to conjure inside his mind with her voice. She began to sway her hips, her cunt lascivious and dripping; every time she felt his breath near her sex or darker hole, she'd move away, make him follow. Every time she felt his tongue in her ass, she'd clench, deny him entry, lock against him, pull away. She felt hollow without him, but he'd fuck her so hard it would hurt, she'd be completely fucked and helpless, and she'd wait for that.

And all the time she stayed with her haunches high, the core of herself on offer, thrusting herself back at him, her cunt red and split, swollen and aching, offering herself up for his fuck. But he tormented her still, rubbing his face into her cleft, his mouth, his cheek, his chin, till her juice coated him, his tongue deep in her cunt.

Madelyn ached and ached and wanted to be filled, but every time she cried out for him to fuck her, fill her, want her, he wouldn't do it. He'd go somewhere else on her body. He turned her over so she lay on her back, her legs spread wide. He reared over her, spread her legs with his hands, and dropped his body onto hers, his hot tight balls up against her wet cunt, the tight flesh of his balls pushing against her spread lips. His cock was hot against her belly, but he wouldn't put it inside her.

And then, "Ohh, Madelyn..." Adam placed the head of his cock against the swollen wet lips of her cunt, "... don't move..."

... she turned against him. Now he wanted to be inside her, Madelyn turned away, she closed her legs, she pushed him away. He tried to force her legs wide to take her, but she rolled on the bed. She rolled and twisted and wriggled out from under him, and he fell face down onto the sheets. She fell on top of Adam quickly, her long body all along his. She ground her sex against the base of his spine, and started to fuck his back, pressing her pubic bone down so her sex splayed wet and hot against the tight muscle where his ass cheeks met.

That wasn't enough, so she wrapped one arm under his neck so his throat was in the crook of her elbow, and she pulled his neck back so his head came up off the bed and his body arched back. With all her strength she held him in the stranglehold, and again pushed her core back against the taut muscle of Adam's ass. To relieve the pressure on his neck, Adam placed his hands on the bed and pushed himself up, pushing Madelyn backwards, but in doing so he lost his balance, and she was able to turn him on the bed so he was on his back.

She pounced quickly, dropping her wet sex onto his breathless face, smothering him between her thighs. Facing down his body, she crouched over him, his hot balls in her hands and she pulled them away from his body to slow him. She bit the base of his cock, the pressure of her open mouth bite a warning to Adam. She was on top now, warning him not to fight, not while his cock was in her hands, anyway. She ground her cunt back against his face, and received her own warning bite all around the top of her sex, her clitoris held in his mouth, swathed with his tongue.

Madelyn opened her mouth wider, sucking a testicle into it, sucking on the egg quite hard, testing for his response. She felt Adam's mouth open wider and yearned for the long pull of his suck on the whole burning flesh of her sex. They relaxed into a tantalising call and response with each other, slowing into the careful delight of eating delicate flesh with their lips, taking the necessary step back from devouring thick, dark blood with their teeth. Madelyn bit gently and her clit was sucked lightly in response. Adam bit softly around the top of her sex, and she answered with a nibble on his shaft.

So they ate at each other's core with delicate teeth, slow and gentle tongues, and warm lips. Their breathing slowed, and their bodies became still, as they each focused on their delectable places; each a perfect prey, their slow mouths on each other. They licked and bit and sucked, but

Maddy didn't take his cock head in her mouth, and Adam wouldn't use his fingers in her sex, so they continued their waiting game, their insatiable, inevitable torment.

Tantalus had more fingers and a deeper throat than these two beautiful creatures, and so they worshipped each other, wanting more, always wanting more, but denying each other completely.

After long minutes of slow eating of each other's core (no-one was counting time any more), Madelyn, because she was on top, raised her head and sat up. She moved herself down Adam's body, leaving his cunt dripped face to cool, and nuzzled the base of her belly around his shaft.

"Sit up," she said, "that cushion against the wall will do," and Adam moved. "There," she said, when his body was angled just right for her next desire.

The unfinished sixty-nine had calmed her, and Maddy was in another, more contemplative mood. She leaned back against Adam's chest, and didn't mind at all when his hands, gentle now and wondrous too, carefully took the weight of her breasts, and his mouth the side of her throat. She leaned back against him, and found a place where her sex pressed down against the base of his shaft, and because his prick was the perfect length, a good length of it could be seen above her belly.

"Look, Adam," she said, "I've got my own cock to play with now." She placed her hand around it, and was astonished by the heat. "Is this what it's like, to be a man, to look at your cock, and touch it?" She turned her head to his to enquire, and together they looked down at the shaft they could see, thick and red with his arousal, the big head a rich plum red. Because her lips were hot and swollen around him, and her arousal had been so long, Maddy felt every twitch of his cock, each pulse, as if they were her own.

She thought his sensation might be stronger, felt from the inside - it seemed to be, if his twitches and gasps were any indication - but nothing could be softer to touch than the velvet smooth skin of the cock head. She touched her own lips and her cheek, and decided the velvet was smoother and hotter.

Her cock jutted up from the carefully manicured heart of her red pubic hair, and its colour, a rich deep red (for his arousal, too, had been so long), was a startling contrast against the whiteness of her thighs and the creamy pale smoothness of her belly.

"Look, my veins are blue," and she traced her finger along a thin vein just under the surface of her skin, in that soft place inside her thigh. "But some of them are purple," and she tracked her fingertip along a thick vein which started just behind the head of her cock, following it along the side of the shaft until it curved under and disappeared.

Adam lay back with his eyes closed, waiting to feel where her exploration would go, as she discovered her lovely new cock that used to be his. His palms pressed slowly against the hot swell of her breasts, her long thick nipples, and because their mood was even slower now, she felt each nerve throb join together and connect up, and she didn't know where his body stopped and hers began.

She took the cock shaft in her left hand, and the heat of it was the heat of her fingers. When she pulled the foreskin right down with her other hand so the skin on the shaft was smooth and tight, a pulse entered her breasts through his hands. When she rubbed the top of the head with her palm, feeling the tiny mouth of the opening there, the hiss of breath by her ear told her everything, and the twitch in Adam's leg told her more.

Maddy looked around at his face again, and loved the way it was tilted back, his eyes closed. There was something in the angle, that if he opened his eyes, he'd see something beautiful painted on the ceiling, a cherub perhaps, or an angel. She looked up at the ceiling, but there was nothing painted there at all.

She smiled, and went back to the slow discovery of her wonderful new cock. She was seeing it for the first time with this intensity, and wanted it in her mouth, her cunt, her ass; but for now, was content with it in her hand and in her eyes. Madelyn knew now, with Adam, they had plenty of time. And there was always Juliette, she hadn't forgotten the girl. The lucky girl, who'd already had Adam. Maddy smiled. She needed to catch up, but she had plenty of time. She wondered where she'd put his watch. Upstairs somewhere; on her dressing table, perhaps. Her house had so many rooms.

Maddy drifted. Adam stirred, and Maddy quickly came back. She was getting ahead of herself.

She decided that the best place in the world for her fingertip to be, the only place right now, was the little ridge of skin just behind the tiny mouth of his cock, where his cock head joined the long shaft. She knew that this little place, if concentrated on properly, would drive a man nearly insane with slow pleasure. She liked the idea of that, driving someone mad with ecstasy, especially this man. It was only fair, she thought, for he'd driven her nearly mad with desire; just with his presence, sometimes.

Maddy was adept with her fingertip, having taught herself since she was a teenage girl to be slow on her clit then fast, in alternating cycles, so she'd come one time, twice, three times, more, during long, self-pleasuring times. And since her time as a young girl, those lithe and nubile times, she'd known clever men with slow fingers, and wonderful women with soft hands, who'd taught her to slow down even more. And she knew Adam, from things that he'd said, and the things that he did to her, that he'd been similarly taught. He'd learned, somewhere or sometime, to move slowly around a woman's body, to give her time to remember, to give her time to forget.

Their arousal had been intense for a long time now, and was building in waves, fast and slow. Maddy wondered how long he might last as she began to stroke his tiny place, the same way she edged her clit. She wondered about herself too, what pleasure she'd want next, before she came, once, twice, three times, more. She held herself off, knowing that when the wave finally broke, she'd drown. Maddy lived for that gasp for air when she surfaced, gasping for breath, nearly drowning.

Within seconds Adam's body began involuntary twitching, with uncontrollable shudders and jerks. Maddy smiled, and continued to stroke in tiny circles. She had a new cock, and he a new clitoris, and it was only right that they share and swap.

"Something wrong, Adam?" she teased. "Oh naughty boy, stay there!" She talked to his cock as it tried to jump from her hand, and she gripped it harder, squeezing the shaft so it couldn't escape. "Ah, that's better, come to Madelyn, there's a good boy." She continued to stroke that tiny place. "There, isn't that nice, do you want more?"

"Ye...esss," he moaned.

"Oh, not you, Adam, I'm not talking to you. I'm talking to my beautiful," she stroked some more, "wonderful," more, more, "gorgeous cock. It's all mine, I think I'll cut it off and put it in a velvet box. Wouldn't that be nice, a beautiful cock for Madelyn?" She leaned her head back against Adam's cheek and turned to kiss him. "You know I like beautiful things." And all the time, she kept up her constant, insistent finger.

Adam was hot behind her, radiating energy from every part of his body, and if Maddy could see colours, she'd see them now, streaming from him. His breath came in gasps as she took his body up into silent orgasms just like her own, and still she kept on with her finger.

"Oh look, isn't that beautiful? Look, Adam, you're making diamonds." Adam's eyes were tightly closed. "Oh, my lovely man, you've got your eyes closed, you can't see."

Madelyn stopped her tiny strokes, fascinated to see clear the bright beads of fluid flowing crystal clear from the little mouth of her cock. She watched closely as several more beads of pre-cum formed, glistening on the head of her cock like beautiful jewels. She gently touched her fingertip to the tiny beads, and rubbed them around the head. Adam shuddered, and Madelyn smiled.

She eased her body back a little, so she could slide her fingers into herself, with a gentle sigh. She played with herself for a while, enjoying her own sensation, knowing Adam was lost in his. Maddy brought her finger up before her eyes, angling it back and forth to catch the light, so she could see her glistening juice. "Look, Adam," she said, "I'm making silver, I'm shining."

Adam didn't speak, but she loved the soft stroke of his fingers down her back.

"I'm very, very wet, Adam. I wonder why that is?"

Maddy eased herself up from his body, and slid to the bed beside him. "Don't move, I'm just stretching my bones." She got up from the bed and stretched her arms up towards the ceiling, elongating her graceful body, stretching up tall on her toes.

Adam gazed at her. "You're very, very beautiful, Madelyn Jane." She heard in his voice a tone she'd never heard, a tone full of wonder, as if he'd never seen her before.

Maddy looked down on Adam and saw the look in his eyes, his impossible depths. She took a deep breath, because she knew she was about to drown. "Are you okay, my darling," she whispered, meaning are you comfortable, but really meaning I love you, but she didn't know the words for that.

She came back to the bed and sat above him, feeling the blood hot heat from his shaft. She slid on him to make his prick shine with her cream, and then she raised herself up, took his cock in her hand, and positioned it between the swollen lips of her sex. She eased the head back and forth twice, to make sure the angle was just right, then Maddy began to slide down onto his shaft.

She kept her eyes wide open the whole time, focussing on the depths in Adam's eyes as he gazed back at her. As she slid slowly down onto him, Maddy achingly and gently filled herself full with her man, wondering why she'd waited so long; and as they made love, she discovered the reasons why:

"I don't know why I do that," he said, as he jabbed the button.

"Stop pressing it then," she replied, as she looked into his eyes.

She tucked her arm in his, as they walked across the crossing. If she didn't actually do that then, she did so now, because that was where she met him and first walked arm in arm. And if she hadn't touched his arm then, his beautiful cock wouldn't be inside her now, and her breasts wouldn't ache, and her nipples wouldn't feel like fire, and she wouldn't be throbbing inside.

"I go in here," he said, pointing into a building.

No you don't, because if you do, I'll never see you again, and you won't make me laugh, you won't make me smile, I won't have your card, I won't know who you are, Mister Cain. And Madelyn couldn't bear the thought of that, so she loved him a little faster, sliding deeper on his cock, squeezing him tighter so he never went into that building at all.

"Is that perfection, that I see," Adam said, as she handed him a coffee.

It is Mister Cain, as I showed you my breast, the inside of me, my beautiful petals, my colours, my long fingers in my cunt, because I really wanted you inside me even then, your beautiful eyes, your crooked smile, and all because of me. Look at me now, I'm shining.

"Are you marking me, Madelyn, like a cat?"

My sweet god, yes I was, my piss around your shoes, marking the ground you walked on. Your cock in my mouth, that first taste of you, scarring my senses forever. I drank you down, later, didn't I, Adam, when you gave me all of your seed? You wanted to fuck that little girl, but you didn't because you wanted me more. Fill me up now, break me in two, because one of me is never enough. I don't love you one time, Adam, because once is never enough.

Maddy slowly fucked Adam, her eyes open in wonder as she sank onto him, her body opening up for him to be deeper inside her. Every bit of her flowed together with him as she took her man inside herself.

"Is she my beautiful gift, Madelyn, who you brought to the garden, the lovely Juliette?"

She was, and mine too, because she filled me up with three fingers when I was desperate in a dirty toilet cubicle because I was already tormented by you; my little Juliette who I think is so pretty and I dress her up like a doll. I like watching her with you. She told me all about you, Adam, how you carried her off to your bed. I was a little bit jealous, but look at you now, all mine. Ooo, that's right, can you feel her in the room?

Madelyn sat high on Adam's cock, grinding down, and she pinched her nipples hard to make them hurt. He reached up and brushed her hands away from her breasts, and cupped them so gently they hurt even more. Madelyn ached inside as she fucked Adam slowly.

"Did you tie her up for me, no ribbons and bows, but so very sweet?"

My naughty Juliette who I can't tame, just like I can't tame you. She's a wilful girl who must be made to behave; can we do that together, Adam? Love her like I'm loving you, can we do that, make her a good girl? Oh my sweet god love me longer, love me deep. I'm an empty space, Adam, fill me up. Your cock in my mouth, you gave up your seed like hot molten pearls in my mouth, oh fill me full, fuck I want you, want you, want you so much, fill me up. So hard inside, ooo, ye...ees.

Madelyn's lust for Adam, built slowly over time with her games and dramatics, crept up inside her as she loved him, and spread itself through her bones like a craving, invisible thing until...

... She stopped moving on him, sinking her weight down onto his thick sex so she could feel the quick throb of his pulse inside her. She stopped in her own small eternity to make sure he was real, all hers; and when she knew this for certain, Madelyn closed her eyes to keep him locked away, and she began to move again. Her darkness surrounded her like cool water, and she fell forward on to Adam's chest and she drowned. Her need for him engulfed her, and Madelyn began to cry.

"Don't leave me alone, Adam, don't leave me." She buried her face in his neck so he couldn't hear her, but she'd whispered it, and he did. And to save her from drowning, Adam's arms were around her and his hands on her back were so warm. He turned her onto her side, still deep in her, but it was different now because he could move too, and like waves on a wide lake he swayed inside her, and she surged up around him, and came. Madelyn's orgasm slid over her, and she felt Adam's lips kiss her tears away.

"Sshh, Madelyn, I've got you safe."

"Don't let me go, Adam, not yet, I couldn't bear it."

"Sshhh, angel, we're here in your house, the doors are all locked."

Adam calmed her constantly, swathing her with his long, gentle fuck; and Maddy didn't believe herself when she came again, languid ecstasy creeping up from her toes to her head, and she came, shuddering in his arms, her sex pulsing around his.

"Deeper, Adam, deeper... oh, sweet fuck, could you love me anymore?"

He moved inside her in a different way, and Maddy opened her eyes and saw his. "Oh my god, yes you can..."

She rolled again, moving under him; she wanted to feel his weight on top of her. She wanted to feel his long length, and wrapped her long legs around his waist, to be loved by him until she was helpless. Adam sensed it, and plunged himself into her, faster now and deeper, the smack of their flesh together keeping time. They moved faster against each other until both of them were surging up to another plateau of pleasure, together, together; and they both burst together, Adam's jets of cum shooting up inside her.

Madelyn felt every throb, and she too gripped and pulsed, and came again, all around him. She collapsed onto him, her weight long and nothing, but even so, he rolled onto his side, still inside her. She nuzzled her sex down on his, to keep him there as he softened, gripping her muscles tight to hold him.

On their sides, they were free with both hands to croon and adore and crave each other, murmuring sweet nothings while their fingertips discovered each other's skin all over again, their cheeks, his chin, Madelyn's throat, the blaze of red on her chest which faded as her nipples went smaller and puffy. They were tender flesh now, so Adam was gentle with his touch, his palms pressing against her breasts; and the ache stopped, and what was hot ice stabbing her nipples became warm melting warmth as she melted.

She took his face in her hands and looked at him with serious dark eyes. "Say it for me, Adam, say my name."

"Ahh, Madelyn Jane, which name? I think I'll just call you Maddy." His voice was low as he said her names, and she thrilled all over, deep inside.

"You perfect man, you know exactly what to say, so I don't have to decide.'Don't press the button, then,' is that it?" Maddy asked.

"Something like that." And he smiled, and loved her all over again.

Sometime during the next time he said, "See what you do to me, Maddy?" And a little later, "Oh fuck, Madelyn, do that again."

Later again, Maddy woke to find him behind her, spooning her body, his hand resting quietly on her belly. She removed herself from his tenderness, looked down on his sleeping face. After a moment, a very long moment because she had to gaze at him twice, she reached down to touch Adam's lips with her fingers. "Do you know, I think I love you, Mister Cain. I never thought that would happen."

"I know you do, Maddy. Now go and have your wee, and come back to bed."

"You bastard," she laughed, "I thought you were asleep."

"I know that, too," he said, sleep thick in his voice.

"You impossible man," whispered Madelyn. *See what you've done to me?*

When she came back to their bed, in her favourite (downstairs) room in the house, Adam was asleep. Maddy curled her long body behind his, and pulled a quilt over them. She found one of his hands and held it in hers, against his chest. And with his other hand, he covered hers.

"You bugger," she said, smiling into his neck, "you're not asleep."

But he was, and Madelyn held him until she slept, too.

In the morning, Adam cooked her pancakes, Maddy wrapped in a thick dressing gown, just watching.

"Fluffy slippers, Madelyn, who would have guessed?" Maddy stretched out her legs, admiring the ridiculous balls of pink fluff on her feet, each one with two great big eyes.

"What? What's the matter? They're silly. I like them."

After breakfast, because the day was warm and sunny, Adam and Madelyn strolled around her garden, arm in arm.

"We need to talk about Juliette," she said.

Juliette

Juliette thought she might hold some sway over Madelyn, with her three fingers reminding the older woman of her need that night in the restaurant. And she impishly thought her little finger and Adam might be entwined, given his willingness to carry her to his bed and his indulgence of her whims.

Individually, she felt confident she could steer their desires, or at least encourage them; but if they were together and she was between them, she wasn't so sure. And that was where Juliette wanted to be, flat on her back with her belly exposed; a little kitten playing with big cats with sharp claws and sharp teeth.

So it was with some trepidation, or anticipation, or even exhilaration (for each gave her a fast-beating heart) that Juliette stood outside her house waiting for Adam to pick her up. Was he Madelyn's driver now, or a co-conspirator come to sweep her away? She stood on the curb as if it was a cliff's edge, and she waited.

A big car pulled up and the passenger window hummed down. "Get in the back," said Adam. "There are leather seats; you can pretend to be O, going to Roissy."

"That's a long way to drive, just for me," Juliette replied, as she slid along the back seat to sit behind him. When she moved the cloth of her dress from under her, the leather was indeed cool and delicious on her bare bottom. She wriggled against the seat before deciding it was far easier and felt much nicer just to splay her cheeks apart and sit as wide-spread as she could. "Can you drive around some bumpy corners," she grinned, "so I slide?"

"Naughty girl," Adam laughed. "Have you been driven by Madelyn, up in the hills?"

"Yes, I have. She wanted me to finger her as she drove, so I did."

She caught Adam's glance in the rear view mirror, but couldn't read his eyes. He turned his attention back to the road, and she slid two fingers between her lips where she was wet already. Juliette leaned back in the corner of the rear seat and played with herself as he drove. "Don't stop, unless the light's red," she said.

"Safe words, Juliette?"

"Yes," she replied, and smiled at him in the mirror. He nodded - so that was sorted out early, kept simple.

"Do you want a taste, Adam?"

"Yes, please." So that was sorted out too, to ask and to answer. Juliette leaned forward and touched his lips with wet fingers.

"Will Madelyn ask, too?" she asked, after a moment or two.

"I think so. She seems to be mellowing."

"That's your influence, Adam. She's not quite as sure as she was, not any more. We might need to change that." Juliette waited for his look in the mirror, but still couldn't read it.

They drove in silence for two blocks before she finally spoke. "You don't need to ask, Adam. Whatever you want, just do it."

He glanced at her again. "I'm not dangerous, Juliette."

"How do you know?" she asked.

Adam tapped his fingers on the steering wheel, so Juliette knew that her comment meant something to him, but still she didn't know what. She kept her gaze on the rear-view mirror, but he was focussed on the traffic now, not her. So she closed her eyes and enjoyed the rock and sway of her body as he navigated the city streets, the soft rush of tyres suggesting a steady pace. Her touch between her legs was slow and comforting, and her nipples were deliciously tight.

After a while she opened her eyes and looked outside, and saw they were moving under an avenue of trees, with purple blossom catching the high sunlight. "We're going to Madelyn's house," she said, recognising the street.

"Yes, nearly there." Adam caught her eyes, and smiled. He reached for the remote to Madelyn's gate, and the big car crunched down the gravel drive, the gates closing silently behind them. Adam parked behind Maddy's car, and got out. He opened the rear door for Juliette, and she swung her legs out of the car. She presented an imperious hand which

Adam took, assisting her to stand. He looked down at her, amused by her airs. She grinned back, impertinent, enjoying his attention.

She pressed herself against him, tilting her head up for a kiss. "Hello, Adam."

"Hello, my love," he replied.

"Am I?" she asked. "Your love?"

Adam laughed. "One of them."

"Tease," she replied, affectionately punching his arm. "I thought I was the only one." Juliette pouted and looked adorable, peeking up at him from under her fringe. "Have you told her, this other hussy who's got your heart?"

"Careful, she might hear you." Adam said, turning towards the house.

"Oh, you two! Stop this outrageous flirting." Madelyn looked down on the pair from the porch, where she had opened the front door to greet them. She stood tall and magnificent in a pair of stiletto heeled red velvet boots, thigh high, revealed by a long slit dress pulled tight at the waist with a wide belt.

"Dress ups. Do you like?" She turned in a circle, to reveal the long naked stretch of her back and a swirl of the dress as she moved.

"Your Sunday best, Madelyn?" Adam asked, taking her by the waist with one hand to dance with her, in a single turn. She was taller than him, in her boots.

"Oh no, Mister Cain, that's tomorrow. You impatient, delectable man."

Madelyn turned to Juliette, opening both arms for the girl's hug. "Darling, come here, let me see you." Juliette pressed up against her in the same way she'd slid against Adam, her sex against Maddy's thigh.

Maddy breathed in deeply, scenting the girl. "Is that a new perfume, Juliette?"

Juliette offered her fingers to Madelyn's lips. "No, the same one. Perhaps it's leather scented, from Adam's car. I asked him to drive in a straight line, but he wouldn't."

"Naughty girl," Maddy smiled. "What is it about cars, do you think?"

"Journeys and arrivals, Madelyn. You should write a book." Adam commented.

"Truck Stop Madam, is that it?" Maddy asked.

"Something like that."

Maddy laughed, her rich contralto laugh that turned heads.

"Come on in," she said, taking them both by the hand. "I've got lunch ready in the back room."

Adam and Juliette both paused to take their shoes off by the front door. Madelyn waited patiently, not touching her boots at all. Juliette put on a delicate pair of slippers so her white stockings wouldn't get torn, and Adam walked in bare feet.

They followed Madelyn down the hall to the back room, passing her den on the way. The room was neat and tidy, the day-bed made and its covers pulled up. The cat lay curled on its chair, but rolled onto its back for Juliette's fingers. She scratched its snowy white belly, which elicited a little chirrup, then a purr. "Does he ever move, Maddy?" she asked.

"Not much," Maddy replied. "Over there, to catch the winter sun. Outside, when it's warm." She pointed to the floor length windows, shielded by blinds in summer; but today, it being mild weather, the blinds were pulled up. The windows overlooked a garden lawn, immaculately cut and surrounded by colourful flower beds, all in full bloom.

Adam went to the window, admiring the garden. "May I wander?"

"Of course," Madelyn replied, opening a door onto a small stone terrace with steps down to the lawn. He stepped out and moved slowly along a path which ran around the perimeter of the garden. She stood and watched him, Juliette by her side. The girl leaned her head against Maddy's arm.

"He's a good man, isn't he?" said Juliette, and it wasn't really a question.

"He is. He calms me," Madelyn replied, but it wasn't an answer.

"He maddens me," the girl continued. "I can't goad him, no matter how hard I try."

Madelyn smiled. "His impossible calm, but you want the storm?"

"Yes. I've seen it, just before he catches it. He wants to drown, but won't let himself."

Madelyn gazed at the girl for a very long time, before touching her cheek. "I think you're right." She paused. "But darling, be careful what you ask for."

"Then I won't ask," Juliette replied.

"I don't -"

"... think that's a good idea?" Juliette finished Madelyn's thought. "He's not going to hurt me, though, is he, this man of yours? So I don't need to ask, do I? Because he won't." She looked up into Madelyn's eyes. "But you might."

A shiver shot down Juliette's spine as she saw Madelyn's response, a sudden darkness and a glint of something else. She slid her hand up the side of Madelyn's dress to find the hard flesh of her tit and its nipple, tight and long already. She squeezed the breast hard. "You're fucking shameless, Madelyn, with your desire. I should hit you up for another three hundred bucks."

"Sweet fuck, you're good. Where did I find you?"

"In a toilet cubicle, Madelyn, with your fingers in your cunt." Juliette claimed her victory over the other woman.

"Look at you, butter wouldn't melt in your mouth, but you know me better than I know myself."

"Don't be silly, Madelyn. I doubt that very much. We're here in your house, you've got the kinky boots on, and I've got the pretty dress. See." Juliette twirled around and her light blue cotton dress rose up high, revealing the tops of her thighs and her virginal white stockings. "And there's a man outside. We all know what we're doing. That's why we're here. Dress ups."

"Clever girl," said Maddy. "Your dress matches your eyes." She smiled, and put her arm around the girl's waist.

"My bra matched Adam's eyes," said Juliette. "He liked that."

Maddy laughed with glee. "He would!"

"He did."

The two women turned to watch Adam, who was walking towards them with a smile on his face. "Look at you both. The Red Queen and Alice in Wonderland."

"Through the Looking Glass, surely," said Juliette, pointing to the garden. "Did you find talking flowers?"

"Camellias, they're quite chatty. And lilies, beautifully scented, but more reserved. They didn't say much."

Madelyn looked at Adam as if wondering what on earth he was on about. Juliette was delighted he so quickly played her little game.

"Books, Maddy," Adam explained. "Alice through the Looking Glass is the sequel to Alice in Wonderland. She climbs through a mirror and finds herself on a giant chess board. There's a garden full of talking flowers."

"Oh, I see. Mirrors I understand; chess, not so much." Maddy didn't want to be totally excluded from whatever it was her guests were doing, but she had the advantage of lunch being ready. She beckoned Adam inside with a waft of her hand. "Let's eat; we can chat to each other inside. I've some flowers in vases, will they do?"

"Perfect, Madelyn. A rose between your teeth, a crown of daisies in your hair. You've seen Mapplethorpe's orchids, no doubt?"

"Yes indeed, and his men in suits. And Lisa Lyon, suspended. That's a particular favourite of mine."

Adam held the pause for two beats. "Of course. Photographers then, not chess?"

Madelyn smiled, and they began to circle each other, once again.

Juliette went to the table and chose a single pink blossom, tucking it behind her ear without saying a word. She didn't need to, because she saw the crease in Adam's eyes whenever he saw something beautiful, and she saw Maddy's eyes narrow. Between her legs Juliette felt lovely and warm. She didn't mind being fought over, she didn't mind that at all.

"My darlings, please: eat and enjoy. I know I will." Madelyn led them to the buffet, but Juliette thought she probably wasn't talking about food.

Their chatter over lunch was light and inconsequential, a passing of time waiting for the curtain to rise. Juliette wasn't really hungry, but knew she should eat, so she nibbled at cheese and some crackers, and drank down two full glasses of water. She noticed that Madelyn and Adam limited themselves to a single glass of wine each, Adam's blood red, Maddy's nearly clear, the palest hint of gold.

Juliette sat between them, and at one point turned her head up to kiss Adam. She felt Maddy's hand on her leg. She held the taste of Adam's wine from his lips, and passed it to Maddy with a light and delicate kiss. Her hand fell back to the filling weight of his groin and she lightly squeezed.

"Time now, don't you think?" said Maddy. "Come up when you're ready, at the top of the stairs."

She got to her feet, trailed a hand over Juliette's shoulder, and walked down the hall. Adam and Juliette watched the slow sway of her ass in the tight dress, and her legs in the boots went on forever.

Juliette reached for Adam's hand, her smaller hand burrowing into his. "Don't let her hurt me," she said, holding his fingers like a small child waiting to cross the road. "But you can."

"What colours can you see, Juliette?"

"A green sun in an emerald sky, and the peacocks are dancing."

Adam nodded, then took the pink blossom from behind her ear and placed it on the table. He helped Juliette to her feet, and in her pretty dress and little slippers she barely came up to his shoulder. But she took her man by the hand and walked to the foot of the stairs. She looked up.

Madelyn

Madelyn stood at the top of the landing. Her dress lay in a pool at her feet, discarded, but the red boots were still laced tight up her slender legs. The rich, dark colour of the velvet contrasted with the pale skin of her thighs, and matched her pubic hair, dyed the same red, darker than usual. Around her torso and hips she wore a twisted garment made of black leather strips, criss-crossing her flesh, leaving her breasts and sex bare. Her nipples were rouged the same dark red as her hair and the boots, and were thick and tight already, pulling her small breasts into hard peaks. Her mane of hair fell in a twist over her left shoulder.

Juliette took two steps up the stairs so her head was the same level as Adam's. Her hand trailed back to hold his hand, and together they climbed up towards Maddy. It was simple theatre but lent an air of ceremony, a slow performance, to the climb. If there was an audience, breath would have been held and pins dropped. But they were their own audience, and entered Madelyn's upstairs room by themselves.

In the centre of the room, facing a mirror between two curtained windows, there stood a curved and dipped saddle, mounted on four slender wooden legs, carved lion's paws on the foot of each one. The leather seat was worn smooth, with stirrups set wide on an adjustable frame. Carefully positioned straps and soft leather pads would hold limbs secure and comfortable. Anyone strapped to it would be accessible from both ends.

Juliette looked at the device, at Madelyn in her costume, and finally at Adam, whose hand still held hers. She took a deep, shuddering breath and stepped forward to study the whipping frame. "I've never been upstairs before," she said to Adam. "I didn't know this was here." Her voice was soft, as if she was speaking from inside a dream.

"Who made it, Madelyn?" she asked, reaching out to run her hand over the contour of the saddle where her belly would lie, the holes where her breasts would drop and be held. She touched her belly and caressed its little curve, and undid the top two buttons on her dress.

"My grandfather, a long time ago, for his second wife, Jane. She liked the maids and he liked the grooms, and together they had the thing made. It's always been in this room, and then, later on, my father had the key. It's mine now, they're all dead." She laughed, and a shiver ran down Juliette's spine. "It's a family heirloom, I suppose. Anyway, it came with the house. It's part of my inheritance."

Juliette glanced back at Adam, who was watching Madelyn through narrowed eyes. She saw a twitch in his jaw. Juliette looked down and saw the thick ridge in his pants. She smiled her own little smile. "Undo my buttons, Adam. I want to get on it, feel the leather against my bare skin. You can ride me, fill me up. Maddy can watch, she'd like that."

"Clever girl. It's why I like mirrors, but did you see the chair?" Maddy gestured towards the viewing chair on the other side of the room. Obviously made by the same master craftsman, it too had adjustable arms and foot supports with straps and buckles, and its height could be adjusted for easy access to anybody sitting in it.

"Very inventive, your grandfather," Adam observed. "Jane was your grandmother?"

"Yes, my grandmother was a Jane." She smiled. "We're quite traditional, my family, keeping names."

"With untraditional tastes?"

"What money buys, I suppose. I went to the best schools, I assure you."

"I don't doubt that," Adam replied. "Head girl?"

"Not quite. Even then, I'd acquired my taste for pretty girls in the junior years, and my parents had to change my schools to avoid rumours. But of course they started, as they do."

"As they do. It's a small town, this city." Adam gestured to the chair. "May I?"

"Please do."

Adam escorted Madelyn to the chair, and watched while she made herself comfortable in it. He lifted one foot and placed it into a support, then the other. With her legs spread wide and her bottom sitting at the edge of the leather seat, her cunt was a beautiful glistening red, made available. Maddy eased fingers into it, spreading her lips wide for show. She offered Adam a taste, which he took on his lips, licking her fingers slowly. Maddy lay back and watched him do it.

"Can I get you another drink, Maddy?" Adam asked, after a long moment contemplating Maddy's show of herself. "More wine?"

"You darling man. Yes, please." She removed her fingers, licking them clean. Juliette caught a hollowed, nearly vacant look in Maddy's eyes, as if she was lost in herself.

Before he went out of the room, Adam went to the girl, leaning down to whisper in her ear, "Maddy's horny as fuck. Shall we pay attention to her first before we start? Shall we do that for her?"

"Three fingers. She'll love it, the slut fuck bitch. She loves it when she's degraded. It reminds her who she really is." Juliette looked across at the decadent woman, resplendent in her chair, all exposed. "I'll be the little servant girl, you can be the butler. We'll undress each other first, though?"

"She'll like that." Adam said.

"So will I." Juliette's eyes sparkled. "So will you - if my eyes don't deceive me!"

"They don't, you gorgeous little tart." He smiled, and she melted. "There's a stool over there. Go get it, so you can look me in the eye." Adam glanced across the room.

Once he was gone, Juliette went to get the stool. She placed it between Maddy and the whipping frame, angling it to provide the best view.

"Thank you, Madelyn, for all this. You've given me things I never dreamed of."

"Oh, I think you did dream, Juliette. You just didn't think dreams came true." Maddy's voice was husky, her lust seeping through her, her desire for the girl growing quietly. "You and Adam, you're good together."

"He said the same about you. Did your ears burn? We've talked about you. Adam's still trying to figure you out. He thinks you don't know who you are." Juliette stood by the other woman's head, gently stroking her hair. "I don't think you do, either." Her voice was low and soothing, and somehow Juliette felt their roles were momentarily reversed, as if Maddy was the little girl, and Juliette her mother.

She pulled Madelyn's hair back tight into a thick rope, and found a band in the pocket of her dress. She looped the band around and made a ponytail. "I'll brush it for you later, a hundred strokes."

"That will sooth me, yes."

"Sooth you, Madelyn?" Adam's voice broke their reverie. "Not now, surely." He placed the wine glass on a small stand within easy reach.

She touched his wrist. "Thank you, my darling."

Adam smiled down at her, and touched his fingers to her lips. Maddy closed her eyes, to keep him there in her mind.

"Come, my love, shall we begin?" Adam took Juliette's hand and led her to the stool, where she climbed up, holding his shoulder for support.

"It's like Bonnard's shop, Maddy, but to be undressed," said Juliette.

"Show her to me, Adam. And then yourself. I like seeing you naked before me." Madelyn opened her heavy lidded eyes; dreaming, waking, she wanted to see him and the girl together.

"I've nothing to hide, Maddy."

"Yet you hide everything, you impossible man," Maddy commented.

Adam smiled. "You just need to know where to look."

Maddy laughed. "Isn't that the truth! I'll keep looking, I might find it."

"But Juliette. Where to start?" Adam turned to the girl.

"Why, at my feet, of course. Where else?" Juliette replied, a grin on her face.

"Cheeky girl. Of course. How silly of me."

Madelyn smiled. Adam didn't do silly. She settled back to watch, her whole body tingling with slow expectation. Stillness dropped over the room like a drug. If there were candles, they'd flicker, if there were lights they'd dim. Outside, it began to rain, light fingers pattering on the windows. Inside, there was no rain at all. Madelyn sighed. "Ohhh god, just show me."

Juliette stood motionless within the dream, waiting for Adam to undress her.

Adam's worship began as it always did, slowly. He knelt on the floor before the stool, and Juliette stood obediently, even though he gave no commands. He reached for the buttons at the bottom of her dress, which came just below her knees. Undoing each pearl from its loop, he separated the halves of the garment, revealing the curve of her hips and her small waist.

The little heart-shaped patch of hair was dark at the base of her belly. Her white stockings were clipped to a simple garter belt, and her breasts were covered by a little cotton and lace bra, also white. Adam stood, and slowly eased the dress off Juliette's shoulders, letting it fall to the floor.

"Exquisite girl," whispered Maddy, returning her fingers to her sex, easing back the labia and running two fingers along the shaft of her clitoris. "Now, your turn. Undress Adam."

Juliette heard her murmur, but couldn't make out the words. Maddy was so quiet, sinking into her own pleasure, whispering to herself in a soft delirium.

Juliette undid the buttons of Adam's shirt, and it too fell to the floor, along with her dress. He stood bare chested, his hands resting gently on her hips. As she was standing on the stool she was nearly the same height as him, so she looked him in the eyes and kissed him quickly, her hands on his shoulders. "Hello, love," she said. Adam smiled.

Maddy closed her eyes. She couldn't bear to see their affection for each other, but ached for it for herself.

"Careful," she heard Adam say quietly. Maddy looked up and saw Juliette kneeling on the stool before him.

"It's a bit wobbly. It's got a wonky leg," Juliette whispered, but the performance could not be interrupted merely because a prop was real.

"It doesn't matter, we won't be here long," he replied. Her fingers were already undoing the buckle of his belt and sliding the zip down. Juliette looked up at Adam's face with an inquisitive look, wondrous at what she might find. She slid off the stool to the floor.

Juliette began to explore, her fingers spread wide on his gut, feeling his heat, the soft hair. She traced the darker line up to his navel, then ran her finger back down that trail into the hidden place behind the cloth. She leaned her cheek against his skin and felt his hands gently hold her head, one hand stroking her hair.

She looked up at him again, and heard Madelyn whisper, "Ohhh, how he holds her, I want to be held like that."

Juliette tormented Maddy by slowly tugging the waist of Adam's trousers down, easing the cloth over the thick shaft of his cock and onto the floor. He stepped both feet out from the pants and stood there nude, the girl kneeling before him, both hands holding the shaft of his beautiful cock up against his belly. She hid the rod from Madelyn's eyes with her hands, giving her the tableaux of a man and the kneeling girl, a slave perhaps, or a sylvan thing about to be taken.

Juliette pressed her cheek against the hot shaft of Adam's cock, closed her eyes, and breathed him in. Her own lighter fragrance rose to mingle with his musk, and she thought of Bonnard and his perfumes. She kissed the shaft, then got to her feet, stepping up onto the stool once again.

Body to body, lips to lips, she pressed herself against Adam, pushing her breasts to his chest. Her nipples were tight in the soft white bra. "Undo me," she said, and meant the brassiere, but didn't know it meant something else.

"Sweet Christ," Madelyn murmured, "her too?" knowing she had to watch. She took a sip from the wine to slow herself, but her fingers trembled when she put the glass down. "Come over here, sweet goodness, come over here to me." Like a mad woman, she didn't know if she spoke the words out loud or said them in her head.

"Do you want to be restrained, Madelyn, when we fuck you?" Adam's voice broke in, and she saw them coming towards her, Juliette leading the man along with her hand around his prick. "We don't want to leave you alone."

"Not alone, Maddy, not like in your toilet cubicle. We want to fuck you slowly, so slowly, drive you out of your mind." Juliette knew the woman's triggers, knew which buttons to push, and she took control now, seeing the older woman sprawled gash naked, her cunt shining in the glistening light. Juliette might be gentle with Adam, but she knew Maddy didn't want that.

"I know what you need, Maddy, and right now that's a three fingered fuck. Ahh, yes, see, you do want that. See, Adam, I told you. Maddy's a slut fuck tramp. She can't hide it. She pays for sex, did she tell you? Three hundred bucks, I'm worth more than that, don't you think?"

Juliette took the straps by Madelyn's feet and bound her ankles to the chair's frame, wrapping the leather twice around each red velvet boot. "We don't need to strap her hands, she's not going anywhere. Not when I do this."

She kneeled before Madelyn's sex, looking closely at the folds and petals there, before taking the whole wet place into her mouth, sucking at the woman without mercy. She tunnelled and probed with her tongue, eliciting a long moan from Madelyn, "Oohh, fuu...uck yes, you little bitch, eat me, take me with your mouth."

"Don't call me a bitch, fucking whore. Look at you, spread wide for anyone to take. Slut fuck Madelyn. How many men have fucked you, all strapped up and dripping? Adam, fill her mouth. I don't want to hear her talk.

"See, Maddy, he does what he's told when it's me. That's right, Adam, let the tramp suck you, slide that cock down her throat." Juliette was fucking Maddy now, her fingers fast in the bound woman's cunt, fucking her fast like the first time they'd met. Adam had gone to the head of the chair, where Maddy turned her head to take him deep into her throat.

"That's impressive, Madelyn, where'd you learn to suck cock like that?" Juliette pounded Maddy's cunt with her fingers, jerking the woman's body up on the chair with each thrust.

In complete contrast, Adam stroked Maddy's hair gently as she swallowed him, giving her an impossible contradiction. Her eyes rolled back as his cock and the girl's fingers overwhelmed her, and she screamed up to her first orgasm. Maddy pushed Adam away so she could breathe, panting and mewling as she came, a long strand of saliva threading from her lips to his cock.

"Cock sucker, Madelyn?" Juliette laughed. "You should have gone into the Gents at the restaurant. There's a hole between the last two cubicles. The kitchen-hands could do with a mouth like yours." She was relentless. "They don't get that shade of lipstick often."

"Again." Madelyn moaned at the idea of it. "Fuck me again. Adam, come in my mouth."

"Oh no, "replied Juliette, "his cum is mine tonight. You can tie me and whip me, but his seed's all mine. It's payment, Maddy, if you're going to beat me. That's what you want, isn't it, to see me whimper? Madelyn with her little Juliette, doing what she's told?

"Not before I fuck you first, Maddy. Like this." Juliette slid herself onto Madelyn's body, pressing her pussy hard against Madelyn's cunt, fucking up against her. She fought and grappled with Madelyn's hands, finally forcing them above their heads, stopping all resistance with her mouth. The women kissed, and Juliette could taste Adam's cock on Maddy's lips.

Adam moved down between Maddy's s spread wide legs, his turn to taste her sex, her lust drenched cunt. He used his mouth at first and was gentle, but Maddy begged, "Harder, finger me, fuck me like Juliette did."

Adam, not to be commanded, pushed two fingers into Maddy slowly, two fingers which he eased upwards to find her G spot, and his pressure began in her cunt. Maddy quivered with her rising pleasure, one leg kicking against the restraint. She gripped Juliette's breasts and pulled on the bars that pierced the girl's nipples.

She pulled too hard, giving Juliette an unexpected and unprepared for pain. "Sssss," Juliette hissed, "not that, not yet," and she sucked fierce and hard on Maddy's tit to remind her who was on top in this moment, finishing with a little bite to make sure.

"Fuck, fuck, fuck," Madelyn chanted, the beat of her words forced from her by the faster movement of Adam's fingers between her legs, and the matching suck from Juliette on her breast. Adam moved his head up to the other breast, and covered the hot swell of it with his mouth, sucking in Maddy's flesh hungrily. They sucked and bit on Maddy's swollen teats like beasts at meat, she'd be bruised in the morning. Madelyn wanted it harder, bearing down on Adam's fingers, grunting with her exertion. "Unhh, fu... uck. Me.. unnh, unnh. Ahh, that's -"

"Let me," Juliette said. She looked around, and spotted a bottle of lube on the floor. She extended her four fingers into a cone around her thumb. Not waiting to warm the lotion, she slathered a thick jet of it onto her hand and quickly rubbed it around so it was slick and creamy, up to her wrist. "By her head, hold her still," she directed Adam.

Adam went one better. He quickly wrapped restraining straps around Madelyn's wrists, tying her to the chair. She was spread wide, her long limbs bent and strapped, the light-brown star of her anus visible below the dark bruise of her sex. Her breasts, sucked red and hard by hungry mouths, jutted from her torso, the length of her nipples thick and hard, long nubs of dark, swollen flesh. The black leather criss-crossed the alabaster skin of her body, and her neck and chest blazed red with her arousal.

"Isn't she the perfect piece of meat, a fuck slot?" gloated Juliette, standing between Maddy's legs, showing her the slicked and glistening hand. Maddy's glazed eyes absorbed what was happening, and she mewled like a small, defenceless creature.

"Perfect indeed," replied Adam, "quite exquisite. She'd make a picture, on a gallery wall, we could frame her. 'Madelyn Reclining.'"

"'Madelyn Fucked,' more like." Juliette knew the crudity would wind Madelyn more tightly, and she saw Adam's prick bounce, too.

"You bastard," Madelyn whispered. "You let her do this to me?"

"Her hand's smaller than mine, my love. Much kinder."

"Sshhh, Madelyn, there's a good girl. Let Juliette do this for you. It'll be the perfect fit. You know you want it." Juliette soothed Maddy, reversing roles once again. Serious now, careful, making sure her fingers and hand were lathered with cream, Juliette eased the cone of her fingers into Madelyn's sex, turning her hand slowly back and forth, finding her way in.

Adam deftly adjusted the height of the chair and stood behind Madelyn, holding the long hot shaft of his cock against her cheek. When she turned to take him into her mouth, to distract herself from the spreading pain of Juliette's entry, he tugged on the pony-tail, no. She obeyed, and felt the heat of him against her face as Juliette entered her body with her hand. Maddy looked down on herself, spread wide in her chair, taken slowly. Her eyes were glazed and her mouth slack, as if she didn't understand what was happening. Her body did, shuddering as Juliette entered her.

Time flowed and swelled as Maddy's body adjusted to the stretch and depth of Juliette's hand, her cunt widening around the slow pressure. Juliette looked down on Madelyn with something like worship in her eyes, as if her hand, buried now to the wrist, was a sacrifice, devoured by the woman's lust and need like a snake eats a lamb.

Adam was silent, his cock rigid and hard, beating up every now and then to a slow cycle of thick arousal, waiting for his time. Juliette looked up into his eyes and saw a deep, dark stillness there. She gave him a slight smile, as if it was a little bit sad the woman between them needed to be tied and bound for her pleasure. Adam leaned forward, and Juliette leaned forward too. Their lips met, and their kiss was impossibly soft and gentle. Madelyn moaned, seeing their faces above her, and tossed her head back and forth.

"Sshh, Madelyn, it's alright," whispered Juliette, and she leaned down to kiss Maddy on the lips with the same tenderness; then Adam did the same, kneeling beside the bound woman, cradling her head in his hands, giving her the impossible contradiction again, a gentle hard fuck and a soft fierce kiss.

Juliette began to move her hand up inside Maddy, gripped tight by her cunt then released. Adam moved around so he was beside the girl, leaning over Madelyn with her head held in one hand, holding her there for his kiss, and his other hand, gentle now on her breasts, back and forth on each one, pressing the intolerable ache away.

Juliette began to fuck Maddy, stretching her, filling her. Maddy's contractions started and her body began to shudder, paroxysms of pleasure surging into her, flowing swollen heat right into her core as Juliette kept up the slow fuck, deep into Maddy, deep to her wrist.

"Her clit, Adam, sooth her clit. This fuck must be nearly unbearable for her, I can't turn my hand, she's gripping me so tightly." Juliette bonded with her lover, woman to woman, every instinct in her channelling through to her own core. Adam was outside this experience now, but Juliette wanted to bring him in, for Maddy, for herself, for the passion that flowed between them.

Madelyn moaned, a long keening sigh beyond words, held in the hands of her lovers, the gentle man and the brutal, magnificent girl. "Juli... Juli... ette," she stuttered, "whe... ere did I fi... nd you, how do you kn... ow wh... at to do?" She shuddered again, another long orgasm rising over and around her, pummelling her body with exquisite pleasure as Juliette slowed her hand and Adam eased off on her clitoris.

Stillness fell over the room. Madelyn's fast panting breath slowed, and her body eased away from the tension of her climax. Adam, his cock red rigid, with a diamond glistening on its tip, moved quietly around the chair, untying the four restraints, freeing Madelyn. She didn't move her limbs, keeping them spread wide as Juliette eased her hand from Madelyn's hot centre.

With a final cry of loss, of emptiness, Maddy surrendered Juliette's hand and the girl eased it from her, cupping Madelyn's swollen and aching core to reduce the loss. Juliette crawled up onto her lover's body, cradling Maddy's head to her breasts. Finally, Madelyn remembered her own limbs, and wrapped them around the smaller woman's body, embracing her. She suckled on Juliette's breast like a baby.

Adam went to the other side of the room, leaving the women alone with themselves.

"No, Adam, come back." Madelyn called for him to return, so he went back to them, embracing them both with his heat. Maddy reached up for his kiss, hungry for his gentleness, then he left her.

"Later, my darling, later." Adam used Maddy's endearment back at her, and it was a promise of something else, later.

He stood and went to the whipping stand, where he waited.

Juliette stayed in Maddy's arms for several minutes, nothing said, nothing needed, letting Madelyn fall back into herself.

"I'm going to Adam now," Juliette whispered in Maddy's ear, "but before he ties me, I've got something else for you."

"What is it, for me?" Maddy asked, her voice still small and unsteady from the intensity of her pleasure.

"I'm marking you, Maddy. I'm only a little cat, but I'll mark my territory, just like you did with Adam, before he was yours to mark." She wriggled higher, supporting herself on the arms of the chair, with her sex poised above Madelyn's chest. With a look of intense concentration, Juliette stroked and tapped her pussy with her fingers a few times, then let go a trickle then a stream of hot piss, which splashed and flowed over Maddy's breasts and down over her belly and her cunt.

Maddy moaned and jerked once as an aftershock hit her, and her eyes glazed in a last sexual surge, aroused beyond hope by Juliette's hot silken flow. "Fu... uuck," she whispered. She rubbed the stream over her with slow drunken hands, bathing in Juliette's liquid heat, soaking in the girl's spray.

"There," Juliette said softly, as if to herself. "I've sprayed both of you. Aren't I a naughty little kitten?" She climbed off Madelyn and stood looking down at her lover's long, delicious body, her raw and fucked-hard sex, glistening in the stream. She looked around, and saw towels piled on a shelf. She walked to them, unfolded a towel, and brought it back to Maddy.

"Don't get cold, Madelyn, keep warm. I'm going to Adam now." Juliette kissed Maddy on the cheek. "Thank you for letting me play."

Madelyn reached for the girl, but she was gone. "Ohhh, don't go. I need someone to hold me."

But Juliette was gone to Adam, watched with lust and greed by Madelyn's eyes. Maddy ran her hands over her belly and mound, then covered her face with Juliette's smell, breathing the girl in.

Juliette Redux

Adam stood by the whipping horse, waiting for Juliette to come. As she crossed the ten feet from Madelyn's chair to stand before him, her whole demeanour changed. With each step, something shifted in the way she held herself; the tilt of her head, the drop of her eyes, the prickle of hairs on her skin. It wasn't cold but she shivered. She stopped before Adam and placed two fingers to his lips in greeting. "Hello, my love," she said quietly, and looked up at him. "I'm here."

His eyes narrowed as she knew they would, and Juliette momentarily wondered what her own eyes looked like as he looked into them and began to fall. She saw him clench a muscle in his jaw, and her smile was so delicate and small, hardly there at all, as she saw him catch himself on the edge. She saw his beautiful eyes, and knew in that moment he only saw her. She had him, then, her Adam, in the palm of her delicate hand.

Juliette dropped to her knees and held her cheek to the hard, hot heat of Adam's cock, and she held her hands still upon his core. She felt him pulse, and kissed the centre of his shaft. "Tie me to the saddle, Adam. I want it."

He took her by the elbows and helped her stand. Juliette placed one foot in a stirrup and climbed to the saddle, lying belly down. She swung her other leg up, and felt the room's air on her sex and the tight star of her anus, her thighs spread wide. She wriggled, and found the holes where her breasts could drop, and she laid her arms by her head. With a sigh of contentment, Juliette lay herself down and listened to her heartbeat, steady and quick.

She breathed in deeply, taking the sweet smell of the leather saddle to the back of her throat, almost tasting a slightly acrid something underneath; sweat perhaps, or tears. She rubbed a hand where her cheek would lie, and the leather there was slightly darker. Juliette knew it was stained from years of falling tears, as men and women before her cried out in pleasure, cried out in pain. With a sudden flash of understanding,

Juliette felt that Madelyn had fought back tears here, perhaps more than once, more than twice.

Adam tied her, and Juliette found she could move her body back an inch or two, so she could push against a fuck or clench one into her. Her forearms too, were loose enough so her upper body could move a little, but not much. A silly made up rhyme jumped into her head, "I can give a little, take a little, and I'm somewhere in between."

"Not too tight, Juliette?" Adam checked.

"Mmmm, nice and tight."

He came around in front of her and dropped into a crouch, his thick cock standing high, urgent for her. He studied Juliette's face, but her eyes looked down at his sex, looking down.

"You're a good girl, Juliette."

Juliette began to moan softly, from the back of her throat. Her fingers reached out to touch him, but he was just out of her reach, and she saw his cock bounce at her movement. She let go of nothing, and her body slumped onto the saddle.

He caressed her hair, standing in front of her so she could see the colour of his arousal, and then he moved away, stepping beside her. Juliette closed her eyes, and her senses heightened, and her limbs went loose. She felt his hands on her hanging breasts, both his hands, and he twisted and turned her flesh, pulling her tits down, stretching her nipples, squeezing her flesh into a delicious, delicate hurt. Her breasts ached and the sensation in her nipples expanded until they felt huge, and was everything...

Then nothing at all, when Adam left them alone, didn't touch them. Then, slap, a thick slap, twice quickly, and her nipples ached and burned with a sharper pain, more delicious, where he'd slapped her. She heard Madelyn hiss with sharp pleasure, then her own cry took over, "Ohh, yesss..."

Adam was deliberate and methodical. He went over her limbs, her left arm first then her right, finding the flesh where her muscle would burn when he smacked her, filling her with heat until her body burned. At first he was slow and gentle, easing Juliette into the caress of her pain slowly, then faster, listening to her breath, slowing her down as he smacked her harder.

Her thighs were a different touch, her muscles stronger, more used to burning from long rides in the hills, fast sprints on the track, so he used a cupped open hand to smack her, covering more flesh each time. Juliette burned inside, and her nipples thickened and her clitoris spread, and her cunt opened wide and she felt so warm and Juliette began to drift and sigh. Adam moved up to the full round flesh of her backside, smacking her harder on those beautiful curves, on her blooming red heat and hurt. Juliette craved for the pain, wanting more, wanting it harder. She cried out in soft delirium.

"Ohh, my baby, you're such a lovely girl, you're my sweet, sweet girl." Adam's voice became a lullaby, singing softly to her as she swayed and began to float, safe and warm in Adam's hands, and Juliette drifted away, away, Juliette drifted away, oh such delicious pain, until her sweet pleasure broke through and Juliette didn't hurt any more.

Adam stood in front of her again, and Juliette opened her mouth for him, taking the head of his cock into her. He didn't thrust, he didn't move, and all Juliette wanted to do was taste him, savour his heat, feel his love. She held him in her mouth with her lips, and her tongue tasted the musky darkness of him, and her only coherent thought was of Bonnard; if he could bottle it she'd wear his perfume every day. "Every day, my love," she whispered. "Every day."

Then Bonnard was gone and Adam was back, slowly fucking her mouth in and out, back and forth until spittle ran from her lips. Juliette gagged as he touched her throat, and instantly she was breath and hot lips as he pulled back and let her swallow. Juliette floated, and in her dream was vaguely aware of her body, Adam and Madelyn wanting to use her for their pleasure while she bathed in her own hot bliss. Adam was hurting her and she was safe and ever so, ever so warm in his hands, where she'd instinctively wanted to be for a long time.

Madelyn came to stand beside Adam, and she whispered, "Juliette, darling, open your eyes, I'm going to fuck you with this." Juliette saw Adam's cock with a dark vein beating, and pressing against it for her to see was a slim, curved dildo, shorter and thinner than Adam's real flesh, made from porcelain just like Madelyn was. It was strapped to Maddy's groin with a simple harness of leather.

Juliette giggled. "It matches your kinky boots."

"Can she do that, baby girl, fuck you with her cock while I watch?" asked Adam, so Juliette knew she was safe. Maddy wouldn't hurt her, not yet.

"I want her to," Juliette murmured, and she'd float between them, Maddy in her kinky boots and Adam with his beautiful cock, and she'd be their girl, just for them. Juliette melted as Maddy slid the dildo smoothly into her. She was so very, very wet, and her delicate body, already burning hot from Adam's hands, pushed against her restraints as Madelyn began to fuck her.

Adam placed himself so that Juliette could take him in her mouth, taking him in as Madelyn thrust, easing off as she pulled back. Juliette couldn't suck, her mouth became an opening for Adam, just as her cunt opened up and was a hole for Maddy's porcelain shaft, and they fucked her to and fro, her body shuddering between them. Above her they kissed, but for Juliette it didn't matter, for they fucked her to and fro and they loved her like that, she could feel it.

Juliette heard a murmuring of voices and drifted in and out of her dream. Madelyn was fucking her harder now, and Juliette thought the woman must be rising into her own pleasure, she wasn't so gentle any more. Adam left the wet of Juliette's mouth and crouched down before her. "Juliette, open your eyes, look at me, let me see you."

So Madelyn fucked her body, while Adam looked after her mind, holding her face in his hands. Juliette liked that, and wondered where her body had gone. Madelyn took the girl hard, the back end of the dildo curved up into her own sex, a ridge of it riding her clitoris, and she fucked the girl's body fiercely to find her pleasure, rising fast.

Juliette remained aware of movement in the room and in her body, but she felt disembodied, as if she were somewhere else, hearing a fuck and wondering where it was. She thought she heard an animal keening, whimpering out loud, and it might have been her, it might have been Maddy, but she didn't know, she didn't care.

She just wanted to ride her horse to Banbury Cross where Johnny could have a new master, and all the walls came tumbling down, and in the garden was a talking egg, and in Maddy's room she scratched the cat's belly, and still she was riding a horse, going faster. Juliette cried out incoherently, and heard Adam talking about colours, but she didn't know why.

She rocked back and forth, riding her horse, and she felt her pussy empty, Madelyn must have gone, all gone away, Maddy had all gone away. Juliette opened her eyes, and saw Adam's eyes gazing at her, so she kept on riding. She heard the snap of a whip and a flash of pain on her thigh, and thought Maddy wanted her to go faster. Juliette cried out so they knew she was in a long tunnel with a bright light at one end, and she was running away from the queen who was chasing her in long red boots, and Madelyn had a lash in her hand, and was whipping Juliette to make her run faster.

Juliette felt a heartbeat every time the crop landed. She felt a throbbing heat on her skin, beating in time with her heart, and there was a sharp sound that somehow seemed connected. She became slowly aware she was moaning and something was hurting too much, and she had to tell Adam about flowers, buttercups and daffodils, oranges and lemons and the bells of Saint Clements, and then she knew she was screaming.

"It's red blood, Adam, it's my red blood. I can't tell her to stop, she won't let me." Juliette cried out, "Maddy, don't hurt me, I'll be a good girl."

"Madelyn, enough, stop now," Adam called out, but Maddy didn't, she kept lashing at the girl with her crop, raising thick welts on her thighs and ass, then blood.

Adam surged to his feet to place himself between Madelyn and the girl, to protect Juliette with his body. He acted without wasting words, nor stopping to reason with Maddy. She had lost her self control; he could see the darkness in her eyes.

"Madelyn, stop," he said again, louder this time, to break through to her; but again Maddy lashed out, this time creasing his back with the crop. "Jesus, fuck, enough," he cried out, hunching his body over Juliette even more, so he took the whip instead of the girl.

"Madelyn Jane, that's enough. Stop." This time, he changed the tone in his voice completely, commanding her to obedience, shocking her into submission. "Madelyn, go to your room, do as you're told. Now." Adam commanded her, and Maddy dropped the whip to the floor. She looked around and saw Adam and Juliette in front of her, Adam facing her, sweat shining on his body. Behind him, she could see Juliette collapsed on the whipping horse, her thighs and back layered with bright red stripes, and on her backside, a single sheen of blood. She'd whipped the girl too hard.

Madelyn looked down at her hands, and slowly unclenched them. She heard Adam's words echo, 'Madelyn Jane, that's enough,' and she knew he'd summonsed her father to make her stop.

"Look after her first," she said quietly, knowing in her heart that Adam would, but hoping he'd care for her too. Madelyn walked from the room, her head still high, her legs going on forever in her magnificent boots. "I'll be in my room."

Adam turned immediately to Juliette, untying her limbs from the horse so she could move when she was able to move. He closely inspected her body without touching her, then crouched down. "Juliette, baby, can you open your eyes, can you see me?"

She slowly opened her eyes and looked into his, seeing Adam's silent depths and his love. Despite her pain, or because of it, he was still aroused, his cock hard. Juliette looked down at his thick arousal, and reached her hand down to it.

"Before it all stops, and I really really hurt, I want you inside me, my love," she whispered. "Will you do that for me, for your little girl?" She swallowed, and winced as she moved. "On the floor, in Madelyn's whipping room? On my knees?"

With Adam's help Juliette slid from the whipping horse and began to crawl across the floor, her back and thighs and beautiful curved bottom a blaze of red, a startling contrast to her white stockings.

"Where are you going, Juliette?" Adam asked, fearing to stop her but watching her every move.

"To rest my head on the little stool, so when you're inside me, I can close my eyes."

"Juliette, my darling, you're not making sense."

"Adam, my love, you're not making love. Can't you see lovely Juliette with her sex in the air, wanting her sweet little pussy all filled?"

She rested her head on the stool, and spread her thighs wide, presenting Adam with her delectable cunt between her pale white thighs. The burning red welts laced around her cheeks and the outside of her legs. Blood beaded from the lash across her cheeks.

"Make love to me, Adam, before the hurting comes back and I'm sad." Juliette looked back at him from under her fringe, and despite her throbbing body, or because of it, she smiled. "Lovely man, you don't have to ask." She sounded stronger. "Remember what I said in the car?"

He went to Juliette, settling down behind her, and he ran one hand down inside one thigh where her skin was smooth and unbroken, two little hollows of flesh next to her lips. Her sex was swollen, aroused, her labia thick and dark with blood. The swirl of her anus was perfect. Adam tentatively put the tip of his finger to it, and Juliette gasped. Her ass pulsed and gripped his finger, but she shook her head, "Not there. In me, Adam, put it in me."

Adam leaned forward and placed the plum red head of his cock at the entrance to her sex. Feeling him there, Juliette pushed back and took him, sliding backwards onto his shaft. She was so wet, and her body so loose from her whipping, the pain still drifting in circles, that she slid back easily.

She winced when the tender flesh of her thighs and ass touched his body, but she kept moving against him. "It's nice, don't stop," but he wasn't moving at all, every movement was hers, taking him in. "Wait," she said, "I'm not right. Bend me over the horse."

She eased herself from him and stood, cupping her hand over her sex to hold the emptiness inside. She limped across to the whipping horse and climbed once more to its saddle. Being unrestrained this time, she was better able to position her body for his access; her legs spread wide, her sex ready for him to fill.

"Fuck me gently, my love, before I really hurt. Put your weight on me."

Adam poised his cock head at her core, and eased himself inside. Juliette cried out like a distant bird calling, and she pushed herself back against him, wanting him inside her.

"Move in me, my love, make me better." Her voice was soft but determined; she was taking him in, easing from pain to pleasure. "Slowly, Adam, don't...

"Ohhh, that's... "

Adam made love to her slowly, careful where he touched her, but she wanted her skin to burn against his. She pushed back against him harder so he'd know she was all right, and to take her. He moved faster as she insisted on her pleasure, and the still room filled with their breathing and the wet slide of their bodies together. Juliette began to make little inarticulate cries as her pleasure built up, mewls of delight.

"Where's Maddy?" she cried out. "I want her."

Adam didn't stop, didn't question her desire, but called out in a louder voice, "Maddy, are you there? Juliette wants you." He kept on fucking the girl, who began to moan with each long, delirious thrust.

Madelyn came quietly into the room. She'd taken off her boots and harness, and was wrapped in a simple silk gown. "I'm here, Juliette. What is it, my darling, what can I do?" She sounded uncertain, a slight tremor in her voice.

Juliette reached out her hands. "Come to me, Maddy. It's not right, in your house, to be by yourself. Come to me, let me touch you." Juliette didn't really know what Madelyn had done to her; but it was all right, Adam was there looking after her as she'd always known he would.

Maddy went to the girl, crouching down in front of her. Her gown fell open, revealing her slender body and legs, and the ripe redness of her sex. Juliette smiled, and dropped her hand down, just as she'd done with Adam. "You've got a pretty cunt, Maddy. Let me play with it, while Adam fucks me."

But Juliette couldn't concentrate, as Adam was pushing faster and harder into her, his own orgasm rising. Lying on the horse as she was, everything was so perfectly right, every nerve tugged taut to perfection, and Juliette began to fly. Her brain, full of swirling chemicals, conjured colours behind her eyes, and as her orgasm blossomed and bloomed, Juliette walked on green grass and she soared high above a mountain.

Adam burst inside her, his cock pulsating, jetting his cum deep into her. Juliette gripped his shaft and she hissed with pleasure as he shuddered over her, his body hot against hers.

And Juliette was a kind girl. She cupped Maddy's sex in her hand as she came. The older woman felt the energy there and didn't want anything more, knowing she'd taken too much.

The room fell quiet; the only sound the continuing patter of rain on the windows and the drop drop drop of water in the down-pipes. After several minutes, Adam eased himself from Juliette's body, his gut striped red from the bleeding welt on her bottom.

Madelyn came up to him, looking at the blood and the thick hang of his shaft resting against his thigh. She rubbed a finger over the blood and ran a trail down the centre of his belly and down the length of his cock. "It looks like she blooded you first, Adam. I didn't quite expect that."

Juliette smiled to herself, a little smile, but nobody saw it. She eased herself off the horse, shaky on her feet, still floating.

"Do you have something soft to put on her, Maddy, something that won't stick to her skin?" Adam asked, as Juliette slipped her hand into his.

"Yes, I'll find something." Maddy tied her own gown around her. As she reached the door she turned back. "Will you stay?"

"No," replied Adam, "I brought her here and she's bleeding, so it's my responsibility to take her away. She needs care, now."

Maddy nodded. "Yes, she does. Of course she does. Give me a moment, I'll find a gown."

Adam held Juliette as she slowly walked down the stairs, her movements unsteady but her eyes bright. At the bottom they stopped, and Maddy came down, carrying Adam's clothes, Juliette's dress and a white silk gown. Maddy carefully helped Juliette into the gown, and tied the sash up with a bow.

"It'll mark, Maddy, with my blood. It will stain, surely?"

"Not if you put it in soak, straight away." Maddy smiled. "I know, it's happened before. Blood doesn't stain, if you're quick."

Adam glanced at her as he dressed, and Madelyn gazed right back, her eyes steady. Neither of them spoke, but Juliette sensed an understanding between them.

"Maddy," said Adam, "when Juliette's asleep, I'll call you, make sure you're all right." He touched her lips with his fingers. "Send me your number. I should call you, don't you think?"Maddy laughed. "I didn't expect that either, not so soon, anyway." She turned to the front door, opened it on its silent hinges, and stood to one side as Adam helped Juliette through. She touched the girl on the cheek. "I'm not a monster," she said quietly. "Not really."

Juliette sat in the front seat of Adam's car, her head leaning against the door post. She closed her eyes and listened to the rush of the car tyres on the wet road, and the swish swish of the wipers as they drove through the city streets. She was getting cold now, but knew Adam would keep her warm while she slept and he watched over her.

They had been driving five minutes when she heard the message alert on Adam's phone.

"Can you check that for me?" he asked, handing her the phone which lay in the centre console.

Juliette tapped on <Messages> and smiled. She showed Adam who the message was from: <Madelyn.>

"We've got her number, finally," said Adam

"Three. I've always known it, her number's three," Juliette replied, holding three fingers in the air.

There, I've done it with...but that's the square root
holding time to ace it about...

Madelyn Redux

"Good afternoon, _____ Partners, Theresa speaking. How may I help you?"

...

"Hello, Mister Cain. I'm fine, thank you. Thank you for asking."

...

"Well, I have to, really. It's our protocol, part of our brand, answering the phone properly. It's a bit scripted, though, isn't it?" Theresa lowered her voice and quickly looked around, feeling guilty about her tiny conspiracy with Adam, but loving his delicate tease..

"Oh no, Mister Cain, I can't say. I'd never do that. She'd -"

...

"God, do I? That's - "Theresa blushed as Adam cut her off, quickly getting to the purpose of his call to save her further embarrassment.

...

"Let me just check." She clicked on the Managers' Calendar, recovering herself with the simple task. "No, I'm afraid she's got this hour blocked out, marked private. I don't... "She silenced her knowledge as to where Madelyn was."Can I help, get her to call you, or check something myself?

"Sure, let me just make a note... which project? Uh huh, yes I... I've got that... yes... yes... that's fine. I'll check those details and get back to you."

...

"And ask her to call you... yes... yes, I will."

...

"Umm, Adam, may I call - "He interrupted her again, almost as if he could read her mind. "Thank you, yes, I will. Adam." She listened for a moment. "Umm, I probably shouldn't... I know I shouldn't, it's none of my business, but..."

...

"Shit, I... oh my God, I'm sorry, I'm... "Theresa was inescapably flustered, but was committed too, so she ploughed on, her cheeks crimson, her hands over the phone, her voice a whisper into the mouthpiece. She finally blurted it out:

"Is Madelyn all right? I'm worried, I.... she's not her usual... God, I shouldn't be saying any of this, but you..."

...

"What is it? About her that worries...? She's flat. There's no life... I mean... she's just not... Madelyn. It's not right, is it? Madelyn not being Madelyn... I can't..."

...

"What can you do? Well... whenever you've been in, she's... I don't know... she's content. For days afterwards.... well, she never says anything, of course she doesn't, but I'm not silly. I can tell. You obviously make her happy and... yes, a happy Madelyn is a peaceful Madelyn, which is good for... well, you know, for all of us. She can be such a bi... oh my god, did I just say that?"

...

"I suppose so, yes... Goodness no, HR? God, never. I'm too much of a scatter-brain to ever be in HR."

Theresa calmed herself as Adam continued their conversation for a little longer, putting her mind at rest, outlining one or two tiny things he might do, reassuring her that no, really, it was fine, he didn't mind at all, she wasn't being nosy. Well, not very, but he made sure she laughed with him, knowing that actually, she was.

Even so, after he ended the call and Theresa played it over and over in her mind, wondering what on earth had come over her to say anything, to even open her mouth; the one relentless image that forever stayed in her head, etched like a commandment in stone, was the way Madelyn had looked at her that day when she'd turned around in the lift.

And the way, a moment before, Madelyn had run a hand down over her skirt and her taut, wonderful ass. Theresa knew, she just knew, that Madelyn was inviting her to imagine that beautiful body naked, no underwear at all; for when she'd run her hand down over her skirt, she knew there was nothing between the cloth and Madelyn's skin, nothing at all.

Theresa couldn't get those images out of her head, so she knew ultimately she'd said what had to be said, because the world wasn't right without Madelyn being content. And Theresa knew Adam could do something about that. Then Madelyn would be happy and she'd flirt with Theresa, and if Theresa was hungry for anything, it was that.

Later that night, in bed, Theresa played the conversation over in her mind once again and thought she'd probably curl up and die, a crumpled heap on the floor, the next time Adam came into the foyer and looked at her with that smile in his eyes, just for her.

Despite the agony of her embarrassment, Theresa came twice that night, her fingers wet in her sex, her breasts heavy and her nipples sore from pulling too hard. She came once when Madelyn undressed in the lift and walked towards her completely naked, coming around behind the counter and dropping to her knees, spreading Theresa's legs apart, eating her wet pussy and pushing a long, elegant finger right up Theresa's tight ass. She'd cried out Madelyn's name the first time she came, and clenched on her own finger, imagining it was Madelyn's.

Fifteen minutes later she'd whimpered Adam's name, but couldn't decide, in her fantasy, whether she wanted to fuck him or suck him; so in her fantasy, she did both. And the second time Theresa came, picturing Adam's cock deep inside her and his mouth on her tit; Madelyn was there in her head, calling her name.

"Madelyn, you've been scaring the kittens. Poor Theresa, she doesn't know what to do." Adam swirled the barista's perfectly formed leaf into his coffee before taking a sip. Dappled sunlight shaded the outdoor table, and the drowsy movement of the mid-morning city drifted by. A tram bell clanked on the opposite side of the square.

"Oh, what's the story, what's going on?" Madelyn asked. "What have I done?"

Adam explained the girl's mortification, telling him of her concern about Maddy's well-being; but for Theresa's sake he didn't mention the accidental near-mimicry, *Oh no, Mister Cain, I can't say. I'd never do that.*

"Oh dear, has the sweet thing got a bit of a crush on me?" Madelyn smiled at the idea of it. "And I thought it was you, her unrequited daddy thing. It must be terribly complicated." She casually swung a high-heeled shoe from her toes, thus drawing attention to her slim legs and the taut muscle of her thigh, as well as her delectable feet.

"Speaking of complications, how is Juliette, after the other night?" Maddy held Adam's gaze, thinking the girl had very possibly got exactly what she wanted from both of them. "And you, so commanding, sending me to my room." She looked at him with a wry smile. "Perhaps it's me with the unrequited daddy thing."

Then, like a cloud across the sun, Maddy's mood changed. "Perhaps it really is me, after all."

"Yes, what exactly did happen there? My back's still smarting - I'm glad you only struck Juliette really hard just the once, you've got a hell of a swing." He paused. "She's fine, by the way. Very teary the next day, but I expected that. Lots of cuddles, and quite a lovely long bath when she came down. Lots of bubbles. And sleep. She's really very lovely when she's peaceful, curled up. I just sat by her as she fell asleep." Adam turned the spoon in his cup slowly, his eyes distant. "Several times, in fact."

"Are you spoiling her?" Maddy asked, looking at him fondly. She liked this gentle side of Adam, liking him without envy of Juliette, liking him for being just who he was.

"Probably," he replied, focussing back on Maddy, accepting her gaze.

"Why not? She's worth it."

"She is."

After a very long while Maddy turned to Adam, very seriously. "Will she want to do it again, do you think?"

"Actually, Madelyn," and he looked at her closely, studying her beautiful, angular features, her high cheek bones, "I think she'd quite like to whip you."

Madelyn's foot stopped rocking her shoe. "Would she indeed? And what about you?"

"I'd watch."

"Would you indeed?"

"I would."

After a long moment, Maddy's shoe began to rock once more.

"The little minx," she said, and sounded quite proud. "Bonnard said she had promise. He was right."

"Juliette?" Adam rang her the next day. "We need to take care of Madelyn. When are you free?"

"Darlings! Are you here to make a fuss?" Madelyn greeted them on the steps of her porch, just as she had the previous weekend. "Goodness, am I under-dressed?"

She was wearing the same tight jeans she'd worn to the zoo with Adam, with a shirt knotted above her bare midriff. Bare footed, with her hair tied back in a single ribbon, she was fresh-looking and relaxed, looking her natural age, without adornment or artifice. Her mask was gone and her eyes were alive.

Adam and Juliette, on the other hand, were both formally dressed in black and white, as if going to a cocktail party or a night at the theatre. Juliette carried a soft leather bag slung over her shoulder. Madelyn suspected it came from Bonnard's shop, and wondered what might be in it.

"It won't matter," said Adam, "you won't be dressed for long."

Madelyn looked at him with a long, slow appraisal. A tiny smile creased her eyes, to match his. "That sounds perfect," she said. She briefly wondered how many games they'd play before she got bored and it all became predictable. At this rate, there would be many dalliances for a considerable length of time. She had no idea what they had planned for her tonight.

Juliette smiled, a coquette in a little black dress. "Hello Madelyn," she said quietly, running a gloved finger across the other woman's bare skin from one hip to the other, circling her navel once. She slowly peeled the glove from her hand, and put her fingers to Madelyn's lips. "Aren't you going to invite us in?" she asked. Of course," Madelyn replied. "Your clothes, you two; you've got me curious."

"Like a cat, Madelyn, ready to die for us?" Juliette asked, her fingers lingering on Madelyn's arm. "Or do you still have nine lives left?"

"Maybe not nine, but several." Maddy laughed. Whatever the pair had in mind for her, she was intrigued and content to follow their lead. She very much liked inquisitive kittens, and Juliette was one of the best; and with Adam in the room she'd be the cat who got the cream, there was never a doubt about that.

"Am I going to be pampered?" She was, and knew it, but -

"So impatient, Madelyn, can't you wait?" Adam removed a black silk scarf from around his neck and trailed it from his hand. "We're not even through the door."

"Oh, you delicious man, stop teasing," but she meant, tease me more.

The door closed behind them, shutting with a satisfying thunk. Adam turned the key in the lock, and a thrill shot down Madelyn's spine.

She walked silently between them on the carpet running down the centre of the hall, hearing the steady pace of their feet on the wooden floor boards as they escorted her into her own house.

"Stop there, Madelyn," Adam directed her. Madelyn stood in the centre of the back room, with its long windows overlooking the garden. She waited. "Kneel down in front of Juliette."

Maddy licked her lips, her eyes went dark, and she knelt before Juliette. The girl looked down on her without a word, and reached for the scarf in Adam's hand.

"Good girl," said Juliette, and Madelyn moaned at the words. She closed her eyes and Juliette made the darkness darker by winding the scarf around her head, blindfolding Madelyn. "There, not too tight?"

Maddy shivered. Her mind flashed back to the first time she'd met Juliette, and she moaned again, her lust unravelling without hope.

"Sshhh, Madelyn, don't be a whore. You give yourself away." Juliette slowly stroked Maddy's hair before twisting it up into a coil, tying it away from her neck.

"Did you bring it?" Madelyn heard Adam ask, and wondered what 'it' was.

"Of course," Juliette replied. "You put it on her; I'll keep the key on a little chain between my breasts." Maddy pictured the valley between Juliette's beautiful breasts. Her own nipples tightened, and she felt heat in the base of her belly. She wanted to touch herself, wanted to be touched even more.

But nothing happened at all, no more voices, no more words. Madelyn didn't move, for fear they'd leave her, her obedience triggered by the simple action of kneeling, being told what to do. Maddy knew she wasn't tied or bound, she wasn't restrained in any way except in her own mind and by her utter desire to be taken by these two, however they chose to take her.

She knew most of it was symbolic, playing erotic theatre and exquisite, decadent games. Even so, giving herself up to someone so completely was unusual for Madelyn. But these two, Adam and sweet Juliette, they were so very inventive together, and Madelyn gave herself up to them willingly. She knew the day would ebb and flow, but had no idea how it would end. She hoped deep inside they'd stay, but wouldn't ask them to. Not this time.

Madelyn became aware of a presence before her, and breathed in Adam's cologne. She felt a slight pressure against her throat and heard the click of a small lock, a heaviness placed around her neck. She felt two fingers placed between her skin and the band, already warm and she thought it was leather. Adam checked it wasn't too tight. Maddy could hardly breathe - it had been a long time since she'd been collared, and she wondered whose idea it was.

She felt the soft kiss of Juliette's lips against hers, and knew the answer then. Adam would gaze into her eyes and take the back of her head in his hand, and she would do the same; and they'd each fight their own desire. But Juliette was younger, still in her first delight, and took what she wanted without question or caution. She might be punished later for her audacity, but that might be part of her plan.

"Call me Mary Poppins, Madelyn. Bonnard helped me fill my bag, and he told me about the first time your mother took you to see him. 'Sixteen and so slender; Juliette, can you imagine?'" Juliette mimicked Bonnard's lilting voice. "'Even then, I knew! Such a wicked girl. Just like you, my pretty Juliette, so very much like you.'"

Madelyn shivered with a thrill of joy. Goosebumps shimmered her arms.

"Oh look, Adam, she's cold."

"Not cold, Juliette, I don't think she's cold at all," Adam replied, and Maddy felt his warm hands stroking her skin, making her shiver again, up and down her spine. She swayed on her knees, her balance shifting.

"Careful, Madelyn, before you fall." Adam's voice was soft, he'd seen her unsteady. She felt a tug on the ties of her shirt, and the knot was undone, the garment pulled away from her torso and arms. Maddy felt her bare nipples harden at the exposure to the air and their eyes, and she gloried in Adam's slight intake of breath. She arched her back, always proud.

"Look, Adam, she's showing off her splendid tits. We mustn't leave them alone."

Maddy moaned as two hot mouths took her nipples in, sucking each one. She felt Adam open his mouth wide to suck in as much flesh as he could, while Juliette's tongue darted and swirled delicately, flicking the nipple tip playfully, teasing her. Maddy felt Juliette's warm hand find hers, fingers entwined; and the women held loving hands.

Adam's arms circled Maddy's back and she was held, kept from falling, in his arms. Her breasts ached as they suckled, and she started a soft, tiny whimper in her throat, "Ohh, ohh..."

"Stay there, Juliette." Adam's mouth left her breast, and Maddy sensed him move behind her. Sure enough, she felt his fingers deftly undo the button on her jeans and slide the zip down, his hand warm on her belly as he did so. He eased the tight cloth down over the curves of her ass and slowly down her thighs. "On your hands and knees, Maddy, so we can get these off."

Madelyn obeyed, dropping down. She stretched her legs out one at a time, to aid Adam slide her jeans off. He caressed the taut globes of her ass and ran his hand down one thigh, avoiding her sex completely.

"That's pretty lace, Maddy," said Juliette, as she peeled down Madelyn's panties and waved them past her nose. Maddy caught her own scent, giving away her arousal.

Juliette tapped her knees apart on the floor, and Madelyn felt the room's air on her sex and ass. Her belly felt thick and heavy as her cunt began to bloom. She pictured how she must look, her sex exposed, her lips slowly parting. She wanted to suck on herself and taste her own hot heat. She arched her body backwards to open herself wide, pushing her sex back for their eyes.

But Maddy was left alone on her hands and knees, naked in the middle of the room. An exquisite wait began, as she wondered what they were doing. She heard a cupboard door open and close; one of them was in the kitchen. The fridge door opened and she heard a liquid pour. Footsteps came back, and a bowl or a cup was placed on the floor near her hands. Every sound became more intense as Madelyn strained to hear everything. She couldn't sense where they were.

She could smell milk in the bowl before her. She whimpered, but knew not to drink until commanded. Madelyn usually controlled her world far too tightly, wound up like a watch, so giving herself up to Adam and Juliette was a sweet, unexpected bliss. In a last fleeting moment of coherent thought, Madelyn remembered she still had Adam's watch in her room; but then she went where they took her. A long keening moan fell from her lips, "Use me, I'm a fuck hole." Her body jerked, a first twitch of intense arousal triggered by her exposure in the centre of the room.

"That's very generous, Madelyn, but really, you must wait." Adam's voice came from the other side of the room. Was he just watching her, like an object, seeing her naked there? Maddy's imagination started to unravel.

Ohh, what was this? Hands ran up over her haunches and up her sides, a light touch from palms, it must be Juliette. Maddy felt a weight all along her body as the girl lay over her, and there, a hot kiss on the back of her neck, ahh god. She turned her head, hoping for Juliette's lips, but instead she felt the hang of her breasts pulled down. Juliette held Madelyn's breasts and squeezed them together, pulling them down. The girl rubbed her palms hard over Madelyn's nipples.

Fuck - she felt a cold, sharp pain, then the hanging weight of two nipple clamps, stretching her breasts. Ahh, that felt good. Maddy inhaled quickly, a quick ssss between her teeth. All feeling centred in her breasts, her long stretched teats, a chained weight between them swinging as she moved. A delicious heat blazed through her body. Her fingers gripped the carpet, holding on.

"Good girl, Maddy. Isn't that lovely, that tight pain in your tits, stretching your nipples?" Juliette tugged on the chain, and Maddy felt a pull on the leather collar as the chain was clicked to it. Whenever she moved her head, her neck, the chain pulled on her breasts. Her nipples felt huge and swollen, and she craved the thick sensation that was in them.

"Now, let me see... " Juliette rummaged in her bag. Maddy mewled in anticipation.

"Oh look, here we are. Adam, come see."

Maddy's heart beat faster, Juliette's commentary priming her mind for whatever came next. Not knowing was delirious, and whatever it was, Maddy wanted more. In her mind's eye, she sat on Adam's lap, his hard cock embedded deep in her sex, at the same time watching herself kneeling on the floor, with Juliette in her little black dress taking things from her miracle bag. Juliette's voice was hypnotic, running a commentary of expectation straight through Maddy's imagination, straight into her sensual heart.

"Good girl, Maddy. Open wide, suck on this." A cold object was placed just between her lips, and Maddy explored it with her tongue - ahhh, a small metal butt plug, she had to spit on it to get it all wet.

"Wait, Juliette, more lube. Make it slide." Sweet fuck, Adam's voice was closer, where was he? Maddy turned her head to and fro, trying to sense where he was. The chain from her neck pulled and tugged at her nipples. Her clitoris throbbed as her nerve centres all connected, but she didn't know where he was.

"Ahh, Madelyn. Your glorious cunt, right before my eyes!" Adam was behind her. Madelyn swayed her hips backwards, towards him. The movement swung the chains on her nipples and tugged upon the collar.

"Fill it, then," she begged, knowing he wouldn't, wishing she could see her sex through his eyes.

"Eager, eager," whispered Juliette, who started to kiss her, to fuck her mouth with her fierce tongue.

"Fuck, are you on your hands and knees too?" Madelyn gasped between kisses, wanting to picture the display in the room; to be her own audience, to look upon herself as she usually looked upon her lovers.

"Yes," breathed Juliette, breaking away from the kiss, "but I'm still dressed, Maddy, and you're naked on your hands and knees..."

Like an animal.

"Madelyn, keep still." Adam was behind her, closer now. Maddy's body jerked, but no-one was touching her. She bowed her head, placing her forehead on the floor, just avoiding the dish. The movement dropped her breasts down, and she pushed her body back up towards Adam, her opening sex and anus feeling the air. And... the cold steel of the plug. Her ass pulsed, and Madelyn waited for the push inside. But no, the cold expectation was gone...

Instead, hot breath and a tongue. Madelyn moaned, forcing herself backwards onto Adam's mouth as he sucked hard on her tightest hole. His tongue fucked into her, and the plug slid into her cunt. She cried out, "Mmm fuck, put something else in me, plee...ase!"

Adam eased the plug, wet from lube and her glistening sex juice, slowly into her hungry asshole. Maddy sighed with pleasure as her sphincter clamped over the swollen metal end, sucking the plug into place. She relaxed and felt the weight of the plug in her ass, heavy and full, filling an empty void in her mind.

"Jeesus, that feels good." She managed the words, only just.

Oooh yes, even better! Adam clicked a chain to a ring on the plug, and Maddy's asshole was connected to her breasts and throat by the weight of the chain. Whichever way Madelyn moved, she sent sensation somewhere else in her body.

"There," said Juliette, "she's all joined up. You can drink now, pet, now that you're all connected together." She paused. "Then we can go upstairs and Adam can get out of his clothes. Juliette wants a fuck." She paused again, then giggled. "We might let you watch."

Madelyn, swamped now with sensation and Juliette's wicked declaration, found the bowl and drank from it, licking at the milk like a cat. The only sound in the room was the sound of her lapping, and the soft slide of the chains on the floor. The heat in her body filled the room and Madelyn was the centre of the world. She knew their eyes were on her, watching her drink, watching the pulse of the plug move in her ass. She spread her legs wider, opening her split, displaying herself, her crimson dark petals blooming like a slow-motion rose. She could smell her own arousal, and wanted them to taste it.

Madelyn couldn't stop the intense feelings swirling through her body; she didn't want them to stop. Adam and Juliette could do anything to her, and she'd let them. Madelyn was no longer in control of herself, but that no longer mattered. They were all in Madelyn's house and she was the centre of their attention, just as she always was in any room; but now she was in Madelyn's room, and they were looking at her. Her first orgasm rippled through her body, unannounced. She moaned in sweet delirium as she came.

"Naughty girl," commented Juliette. "You didn't ask if you could come."

"It's nice to see though, isn't it?" observed Adam. "Mind you, it's usually her own fingers in her pussy, not visions in her mind. We should start counting."

Madelyn felt a slide of something on a cheek of her ass, and guessed it was a pen, marking her first orgasm of the day.

"Is her ass big enough?" asked Juliette. "You know she's a slut, once she gets going."

Adam laughed. "Well, that's not something you hear every day, is it Maddy? You with your taut, perfect cheeks."

Madelyn couldn't reply. She was falling into a place where she was just an object for their eyes, a plaything for their minds, holes to be filled, places to be fucked. She no longer cared what they did; she just wanted them to do it. Her sense of self and who she was, was slowly fading.

"Stand up, Madelyn." Juliette tugged on the chains, pulling Maddy to her feet.

She swayed, and felt herself being caught by Adam. "I've got you, love."

Madelyn nearly fell, hearing his endearment.

"You've told her, then?" Juliette's question was asked in a soft voice.

"She knows, but I say it anyway. She's not used to love; it's a four letter word." Adam was matter of fact about his feelings.

"Don't forget me," said Juliette, claiming her place alongside Maddy.

"I won't," he replied.

"Better not," said Juliette.

"Wouldn't dare."

Maddy heard Juliette's delighted laugh at his playful reply. She wanted them both, to be fucked mind and body by Adam and by Juliette. Her rational mind was being torn apart by the mixture of sensual pleasure, intimacy beyond measure, and the dispassionate way they spoke about her, just an object for their lust, but at the same time, loved.

"Can you walk, Maddy, if you can't see?" Juliette was solicitous. They slowly moved down the hall, the weight of Madelyn's chain dragging on her asshole and breasts, an exquisite inter-connected sensation. She imagined how she must look, walking between Adam and Juliette, chains swaying slowly from her breasts and between her legs. She was theatre, a stage prop, a fuck place to be filled.

They slowly climbed the stairs until she stood in the centre of her room. Madelyn felt disembodied, she no longer knew who she was.

Juliette knew exactly who she was, and what to say.

"Adam, what shall we do with our lovely, elegant toy, our luscious, porcelain doll? What do you think she'd like first?"

"It's not what Madelyn wants, it's what we want that matters now."

"What Juliette and Adam want, is that it?" Juliette stood behind Madelyn and ran a hand over her body, feeling the wetness between Maddy's legs, hefting the weight of the plug up into her tightest place. "What Adam and Juliette get, hmmm?"

"Stay there, Maddy. Don't move." Adam's voice came from a distance, and Maddy felt Juliette move away. Footsteps. She turned towards his voice, but could see and hear nothing. She strained to hear movement in the room, anything that would give her clues as to where they were, but they were utterly silent now.

What was that? The sound of a zip. She imagined Juliette crouching before Adam, sliding the zip of his pants down, exposing the thick meat of his cock the same way she had that evening at the truck stop. Her mind fed her the memory of his cock sliding into her throat, her vivid lipstick marking the shaft in crimson circles as she crouched before him, her hands resting on his thighs.

She remembered her hot gush of piss and the way she'd marked Adam, scenting him like a cat. And thinking of piss, her memory flashed onto Juliette crouching over her, the girl's hot stream bathing her body. She moaned, and stretched out her arms in open supplication in the direction she thought they were.

"Are you all right, my love?" she heard Adam ask, and she wanted to curl up beside him, her head on his thigh, her fingers curled round his cock. She'd take him between her lips lovingly, and suck him till his juice came and filled her mouth. She swallowed to make room, and her saliva ran to mix with his juice. Her sex ached, and she nearly fell. She wanted him to stroke her hair and kiss her cheek and put his fingers in her mouth, and put his hands around her neck and squeeze, and bite her nipples and suck the flesh of her neck. She wanted him to crawl up inside her and live in her cunt forever. Her heart beat hard and she quivered.

"Elegant Madelyn, she'd better come here, don't you think?" How could Juliette be so kind? She wanted to be kissed and loved by the girl, and suckle on her breasts. She wanted to slide her finger between the young woman's tidy lips and spread the wings of her sex to find the little purple bud of her clitoris like the heart of a tiny flower, and suck it between her own lips and lick it with her tongue, and Juliette would link her fingers through hers and stroke her hair and kiss her cheek and put her fingers in her mouth and bite on the flesh of her neck. She wanted to suck on Juliette's breasts and be nursed by her like a baby.

"Lie back," she heard Juliette whisper, and thought she meant Adam. "Ooo, is that for me, you beautiful man," and Maddy knew he was naked. She wanted his shaft deep inside her, fucked fast on her back, his powerful body above hers, loving her so sweet and so slowly. But Juliette had said, "Lie back..."

"Let's undo these." Juliette was right beside her. Madelyn felt painful relief as the nipple clamps were quickly removed. A tight jab of pain shot into her breasts, pushing her nipples ice hard from inside her chest as the numbness cracked open, and she hurt. Her tits ached, and she wanted them to be clamped again, to provide another layer of pain to sooth the absence of the first. She felt a hot mouth on one breast and the hot press of a palm on the other, as Juliette soothed her.

"Take it out and give it to me." Maddy knew Juliette meant the plug from her ass. She bent her legs, shaking, and reached between her thighs, easing the plug from her asshole. She moaned as the thick heavy weight left her with emptiness deep inside, and all she wanted was to be filled again, thick and full. She wanted Adam's cock in her ass, long and pumping and filling her deep till she moaned.

Juliette was kind, and cupped her sex and her hot empty hole in the palm of her hand, and she felt the beat of her heart deep inside the hot swell of herself, as Juliette held her.

"Do you want to see, Madelyn?"

Of course she did.

But of course she didn't.

She didn't want to choose, but Juliette did it for her. Maddy felt hands behind her head undoing the knot of the scarf, and the cloth untwisted from her head and eyes, and Madelyn could see in her room. In front of her, lying on a mattress underneath a window, Adam lay naked, resting against a pillow. He was watching her, lazily caressing a nipple with his fingers, his cock long and hard up against his gut.

"Hello Madelyn." He smiled at her with quiet lust in his eyes, and she knew he was hard for her. "Bring her over here, Juliette. I want her on my face."

Beside her, Juliette was still fully clothed, her black dress enticingly tight on her curves. The girl looked up at her with a mischievous glint in her eyes. "Come on, Maddy. You can undress me while we fuck Adam. That would be nice, don't you think?"

Maddy didn't know what to think. Adam and Juliette were filling her mind with an overwhelming mix of control and expectation, intense intimacy and a casual, voyeuristic disregard; and they'd pushed her to do things she usually wouldn't do. She vaguely, to the extent she could string thoughts together, realised they were doing to her what she normally did to them; placing her in their erotic tableaux rather than the other way around. She didn't know who she was.

Juliette tilted her mouth up for a kiss. Maddy was hungry for the girl and held her tightly, enjoying the rough scrape of the dress against her own naked skin. The sensation of cloth against flesh was all there seemed to be, the noise of the rub magnified a hundred times, and she wondered where everything else had gone.

She felt disembodied, sensation coming from all around her as if her mind could no longer manage the entirety of her arousal, and was breaking it down into tiny bits, each one a moment of bliss that lasted forever. She caressed the swell of Juliette's bottom, and tried to slide hands under the cloth of her dress, but Juliette brushed her hands away. "Not yet, Madelyn; so eager!"

"But you're so touchable, Juliette. I can't keep my hands off you."

"But what about poor Adam. We mustn't ignore him."

Maddy looked across to him, but he was no longer looking at the women. Instead, he was casually curling his hand up and down the shaft of his cock, his eyes closed.

"See," remarked Juliette, "he's bored."

"How dare he!" Madelyn looked down on Adam, knowing instantly that this was all one decadent, luxurious, magnificent game; and it was now someone else's turn to be the centre of attention. She laughed as she saw Adam's sly smile, and turned to Juliette with delight. "You two, you're wonderful, you know that?"

"For fuck's sake, Madelyn, will you stop talking about it and get yourself over here. We can talk about it later, if you must."

"Look who's impatient now?" Madelyn took Juliette by the hand and walked over to Adam. She stood over him, directly above his head, with her feet on each side of his shoulders. She looked down and saw his lazy smile as he looked up at her core. "Better than cherubims on the ceiling, Adam?"

"You've said it yourself, Madelyn. Perfection, don't you think?"

"What about me?" asked Juliette, lifting the hem of her dress to the tops of her thighs, so she too could stand above Adam, her feet on either side of his hips.

"You know it too, Juliette. Peaches and cream, my darling, peaches and cream."

"You're only saying that because of the view. Not because of the taste." Juliette smiled, dipping a finger between her lips, giving Madelyn a taste of her honey, then a kiss.

Madelyn was hungry for the girl's mouth, and her ass still ached from the absence of the plug, and she still wanted the tight clamp of pain on her breasts. The pull of the chains had been exquisite, and she didn't want them to be gentle, not yet.

"Bite my breasts. Hurt me." A switch flipped in her head, and she didn't want to take control, not yet. "Fucking hurt me."

There was silence in the room for a very long time. Madelyn trembled, wondering which one of them would sense her deepest desire first, who would stop playing games, who would go where her lust unravelled. She thought either of them could do it, but she wasn't sure who would step forward first.

"You want to be bitten?" asked Juliette. "I'll eat you alive!"

Adam glanced up at the girl, surprised by the venom in her voice, but Juliette gently touched his hip with her foot as her way of saying, 'It's okay.' Her performance was for Madelyn. She leaned forward to the waiting woman and placed a hand high up against her throat, under her jaw.

"You whipped me till the blood came. I can't wait to taste your flesh." Juliette squeezed her fingers against Madelyn's throat, and whispered, "You hurt me, Maddy. I'll hurt you, too."

Juliette ran her tongue up the side of Madelyn's neck and dug her teeth into the other woman's sweet, smooth flesh, eliciting a moan of pleasure triggered by the quick bite. A shudder ran through Madelyn as Juliette shifted and sank her teeth in again, ensuring the bite was wide enough that the other woman's flesh wasn't pinched, nor her skin broken, but leaving dark, livid marks on her throat each time.

Juliette pushed Madelyn away from Adam, forcing her down to the floor, on her back. With one hand still against the woman's throat, she continued her assault on Madelyn's breasts, tasting her brutally, leaving Madelyn quivering and helpless, utterly dominated. Adam rolled to one side and watched, his hand still slow on his cock.

"Show me the marks, Juliette, where you've bitten her." Adam's voice was low and husky, rough from the back of his throat. Maddy heard an edge to it she'd not heard before, and wanted his mouth on her skin. He moved closer, and she felt the soft warmth of his mouth where, moments before, Juliette's sharp little teeth had been.

His mouth on her throat was gentle at first; soothing the heat Juliette had sucked up to the surface of her flesh. But he became more forceful, bearing down on her neck with the steady weight of his fingers, and Madelyn was held in a tightening stranglehold. Behind her eyelids, dull light shimmered red, pulsing with her heartbeat.

She tapped twice on his hand, and Adam released her throat and moved away.

"No, don't go. Stay with me." Madelyn whispered to Adam, scared he'd leave her.

"I think she wants you, Adam." Juliette lay down beside Madelyn, laying her head on the older woman's shoulder. She slowly stroked around the bruises she'd made on Madelyn's skin, as if curious how they'd got there. She cupped Maddy's breast with her other hand and lazily ran her palm over the long, engorged nipple. Maddy pushed her torso upwards, craving the velvet smooth rub of Juliette's palm over her tit.

Adam moved around to Maddy's other side, and he too lay with his head on her shoulder.

"I think," replied Adam, "that Madelyn quite likes the idea of both of us here in her room." He kissed a breast and cupped Maddy's sex in his hand. "But she can't make up her mind who she wants first."

"Both of us then, don't you think?" asked Juliette, running her fingers gently down Madelyn's throat.

"On the reclining chair, then, so she can't move," said Adam, rolling to kneel beside Maddy.

Madelyn closed her eyes, picturing herself spread wide, Adam between her legs, Juliette higher up. "Will you fuck me, Adam," she whispered, as if that was some inconceivable thing she didn't deserve, because if they were tying her down, was she bad? "I'm a good girl really, don't hurt me. Not any more, I can't bear it."

Memories flickered through Madelyn's head, but she couldn't pin any of them down. "You'll have to carry me. I don't think I can walk."

Adam took her in his arms and Maddy looked up at him to make sure he loved her, because it was a long way to fall if he didn't.

He placed her gently onto the cushions of the chair and stood in between her legs. He moved forward, pressing the base of his shaft up against the lips of her sex. Madelyn wriggled her body down, wanting the hot feel of him against her skin while she watched Juliette undress.

The girl was efficient and unaffected - she knew she was pretty, and she liked it when people looked at her, devouring her with their eyes. She stood slightly behind Adam so both she and the man were in Maddy's line of sight. She crossed her hands to the hem of the little black dress and swiftly pulled it up over her head. Because she was a minx and knew Maddy was watching, she turned around to show the woman her back. Then, quite deliberately, she bent down to touch the floor.

The movement revealed the pink crack of her sex and the light brown bud of her asshole, deliciously centred within the taut curves of her cheeks. She stayed motionless like that for a long moment, for no other reason than to let Maddy look.

Whilst she was bent over, Juliette unclipped her delicate bra from the front, so that Maddy could anticipate the sight of her delectable breasts, with a key on a chain in between them. Juliette straightened herself, still facing the other way. "Look, Adam," she said, "I've got my blue bra, the one that matches your eyes."

She turned around, and Maddy gasped when she saw Juliette's lovely breasts, her mind all tormented because Juliette had worn the bra for him, not her, and she so much wanted to be jealous. But Adam's balls were hot against her cunt, so she couldn't be jealous at all. Maddy moaned, her mind and emotions tugged this way and that by these two, and she couldn't think what they'd do next.

"Will it fit Maddy, your bra?" Adam asked. "I'd quite like her lingerie to match my eyes. It would be the height of accessorising, don't you think?" He looked down at Madelyn lying before him. "On my beautiful porcelain doll."

Maddy's skin prickled, the suggestion to be so objectified pulsing right to her centre. Her reactions were subliminal, as if Adam had direct access to her autonomic nervous system. Her mindfulness evaporated, and she craved any suggestion he'd make to her. She wanted to be empty, without thought, without self, and for Juliette and Adam to fill her up with their own lust and desire. It wasn't often that Madelyn allowed herself to be a fuck-toy, but she wanted to be fucked and taken, to be played with, teased and tormented, by these two. Madelyn didn't want to exist, except for them.

"We really must take you to Bonnard," Juliette said. "You'd be a clothes horse for him to match up with Maddy. He'd be in heaven." She giggled. "He'd want to measure you up."

Madelyn just wanted Adam to fuck her, fill her empty, aching body full up; she didn't care what colour the bra was, nor where Bonnard's fingers might go.

"Let me see," said Juliette, sliding the flimsy garment under Maddy as she lay there, and clipping it up between her breasts. "Oh look, Adam, she doesn't fill it quite like me, but she looks rather lovely, don't you think?"

"I keep saying it, she's perfection." He looked down on Madelyn spread before him, her long slender body sliced with the dark blue of Juliette's bra barely covering her thick nipples and hard tits. He took the crooks of her knees in his hands and eased them up, offering himself the slit of her sex and the darker bruise of her ass. "I think," he said, putting actions to his words, "that I'd quite like to fuck her, to be inside her now."

Madelyn, expecting a long tease and a slow entry, jerked with sudden pleasure as he slid straight into her, a deep fuck and ever so quick because she was so incredibly wet. She moaned with the unexpected, swift sensation as his heavy balls pressed into her, "I didn't think...."

"Sshhh, Madelyn, don't talk." Juliette kissed her, then climbed up onto the chair, facing Adam. She kissed him, leaning her weight onto his shoulders, then lowered her sex onto Madelyn's mouth to silence her completely. "Eat me, Maddy, make me squirm. Adam might fuck you, if you're a good girl and make me come."

Madelyn's sex was filled with Adam's thick cock, but his self-control was absolute, he didn't move. Maddy wanted to be fucked utterly senseless, fucked right apart by this man who'd flirted with her, been sucked by her; who'd fucked her downstairs in her den, fallen asleep in her arms, then loved her again in the morning. This beautiful, delicious man inside her, oh good god, she wanted him to move...

But Juliette's sweet pussy was on her mouth, the tidy rosette of her anus right before her eyes, so Madelyn began to lick and to probe with her tongue, and was rewarded with Juliette's quiver. "Oh, fuck yes, Madelyn, there... right there... oh my god, don't stop." The girl bucked, and fell forward onto Adam's shoulder, and he held her in his arms while Madelyn ate her out. "Adam, te... ell Maddy no...ot to stop."

Adam began a gentle slow sway of his hips, a sliding slow fuck deep into Maddy. She licked Juliette faster and deeper until the girl began to shudder and shake, and Maddy knew they were both going to come, it wouldn't be long now. She reached up for Juliette's hot breasts and cupped them in her hands, and Adam began to fuck her faster, he could no longer wait.

Fuck, hard fuck, they fucked; Adam's thrusts entering Maddy's cunt hard, her legs spread wide with a delicious stretch high up in her thighs, her sex wide, her aching body filled by her man's beautiful, beautiful cock; and her mouth filled by her girl's beautiful, beautiful pussy, lascivious and sliding wet.

For every cock surge into Maddy, Adam's long prick fucking her, she thrust her tongue up into Juliette's pussy as deep as she could, fucking her. Juliette pressed her sex backwards, nearly smothering Madelyn, who gasped. Juliette moaned, and fucked Adam's mouth in turn with her tongue. His balls slapped against Madelyn's open sex as he shafted her quickly, shafted her fast, the wet sound of their flesh slicking and sliding, their skin hot and her juices creaming around him.

Juliette changed the angle of her body, rising up first then easing herself forward just an inch or two, leaning her weight on Adam. Her message was simple, she wanted Madelyn's tongue in her dainty asshole. Maddy thrust her tongue deep in, probing the tight, muscular channel, forcing her mouth up against the resistance there. Juliette began to whimper, and she wrapped her arms around Adam's neck, clinging on.

Suddenly Adam stopped moving, and Maddy felt him take three huge, shuddering breaths, willing himself to hold back. She clenched her muscles tight to grip him and help him stop. He gripped the hard cheeks of Madelyn's ass and stopped himself coming, pulling her body right up against his groin, burying himself deep inside her.

"That... was close," he whispered; and Madelyn loved him then, because he wanted to be inside her forever.

Juliette though, she was nearer, she was quickening, she was going to come. Adam stayed still inside Maddy as their hands, fingers and mouths pleasured the girl.

Juliette's fingers dropped down to her clit, and with her own special flicker she urged up her orgasm with a low, keening sigh, her body shuddering uncontrollably as she frigged herself. "Finger fuck me, Maddy," she cried out, and Madelyn did; one lick of her finger to slick it with spittle, then one firm, swift push into Juliette's tight, hot asshole. "Faster, fuck, fuck, fuu...uuk," and with a high-pitched squeal, Juliette came.

Madelyn felt the girl's tight channel squeeze her finger, pulsating as the orgasm ripped through her. She slowly withdrew the finger from Juliette's asshole, and put it to her nose to inhale a musky scent, underneath the honey taste of the girl's sweet pussy. She savoured the mix of scents, but wasn't satisfied and she could still breathe, so she pulled Juliette's ass down onto her face until she couldn't take another breath, and she was happy then, being smothered by the girl's sweet flesh.

And her sex gripped Adam, he was inside her still, not moving while they enjoyed the ripples still pulsing through Juliette. The girl somehow managed to crawl off Maddy and slide to the floor, where she lay with her hand cupped between her legs, clenching her thighs together. "Mmmm," she murmured, "that was a little bit nice."

The stasis broke and the room was silent, the smell of their sex hanging in the air, like the smell of sweet plums fallen to the ground in an orchard after rain.

"Make love to her, Adam; she's been waiting a long time."

Juliette got to her feet, and moved to kiss Maddy, gently tasting her lips, her mouth, kissing the taste of her own juices on the other woman's face. She held Maddy's head with both hands, slowly stroking her hair, caressing her softly like a child. She kissed Maddy's forehead and temple and cheek, her lips light like butterfly's kisses. Madelyn responded, her kisses soft too, she was long gone past hardness and hunger, she just wanted to lie on clouds with her kitten and her delectable man, to be loved forever, then more.

"Love Maddy slowly, Adam, there's no need to rush. I've got you here with my words; I'll tell you what to do."

And Juliette told Maddy and Adam a story, her light voice lilting and laughing between them, urging them up, slowing them down. She would lean down to kiss Madelyn, then turn her head up for Adam's mouth and kiss him; and between the kisses she murmured and whispered, telling them a story about a man and a woman and a princess they found in a garden.

She told them how the pretty girl liked to take her clothes off, and didn't she look delicious and wasn't she lovely, and look how her nipples grew hard. And, ohhh, Madelyn, that lovely hard cock in your cunt, how would it feel if Adam began to move back and forth inside you, wouldn't that feel wonderful? And it was, because Adam started to move inside her again because ohh, Madelyn, you're just so wet, you naughty girl, you're just so very wet, let me see and taste and touch...

So that's what Juliette did, while Adam moved inside Maddy, and she didn't know who she was, one moment Juliette's voice inside her head then a hot wet tongue lightly pushing into her ear, little teeth nipping her earlobe and Adam's hot mouth on her neck, and Maddy lay in bliss between them, Adam's long cock inside her, sliding to and fro, and was Juliette right down by her belly, watching his shaft slide in and out, and was that Juliette's finger softly pushing against her other hole, and was the girl gazing at her there?

And all the while Juliette talked about the lovely, languorous fuck and her commentary was wonderful because without her voice Madelyn wouldn't know where she was, but she knew Adam was inside her and he was moving faster, and Juliette was kissing her harder and biting on her nipples and Maddy's breasts felt huge and heat was spreading over her body, and she heard a moaning grunt in the room, and Maddy realised it was her own moan, her breath coming in deep exhalations, as every thrust pushed air from her lungs and Adam was fucking her faster...

And Madelyn started the climb to the top of the stairs where she would go into the darkened room and a voice would say, Madelyn, be a good girl and lie on the chair and close your eyes and everything will be all right because I love you, love you, love you and with a silent, open mouthed scream she'd come and her body would shudder and her mouth would bite down on flesh and it was her own arm and...

"Maddy, it's okay, you're with Adam, you're safe." Juliette's voice released her and Madelyn came, her sex clenching Adam's long, beautiful cock, and her orgasm pulled the seed up from him, and it was his voice she heard in her head.

"Ohhh, fuck, I'm coming... Madelyn, take me, oh fuck," and Adam came hard inside her, kissing her passionately, wanting her, Maddy, so much; and Madelyn smiled as he came, wanting her.

She panted, getting her breath back, feeling Adam soften inside her, his cum and her juice a warm trickle down over the crease of her thigh, hot and sticky against her tightest hole. She wrapped her legs around his waist, "Don't go, you lovely man, stay with me."

Madelyn reached for Juliette's hand, and the girl held them both, her lithe body sliding half on top of Maddy, half under Adam, so she was cuddled between them.

"Juliette, how did you know what to say?"

"I'm clever, Maddy, remember. That's why you found me."

"But you knew. You knew exactly what to say and do."

"Isn't it obvious, Maddy? You needed a bit of darkness with your sex, that's all. Doesn't she, Adam?"

Adam was still soft inside her. "And to feel safe. We keep you safe, Maddy." He gently eased away, and she cupped her sex where he'd been.

Safe from myself, she thought, and was grateful.

"Will you both sleep with me tonight," she asked, "in my bed?"

Maddy saw something flicker between Adam and Juliette and guessed that they had gone to his bed too, in his room, that it meant something special.

"In your room, Madelyn?" Juliette asked, taking the key from around her neck and undoing the little padlock on the choker around Maddy's throat.

"Yes, in my room."

Madelyn walked between them into her room where, eventually, they slept until morning. During the night they rolled and turned, and there was always one of them in the middle, held safe in the arms of the other two. Maddy's cat came in and curled up on a chair, and he made four.

Juliette rang Adam a week later. "Can I stay with you for a while? My house-mates are driving me nuts."

"It can't be forever," he replied.

"I know that," she said. "Just until I'm gone."

Theresa

< Theresa, please put aside an hour in MS03 next Thursday, any time that suits. I'd like to go over the mentoring program with you. I think you'll be an excellent candidate. Let me know the booked time. Thanks, Madelyn. >

Theresa kept opening Madelyn's email throughout the week, excited that she'd been chosen for the program, not knowing what to expect.

On Thursday she wore her best suit, knowing she needed to impress. She'd seen Madelyn often enough around the office to see exactly how she dressed and accessorised whenever she had a client or a staff meeting, and Theresa decided that a discrete cleavage would be best. She was bigger breasted than Madelyn and could never go bra-less to work. She envied the older woman, who often did go without a bra, and the way she ignored men's looks when she did.

Theresa was a minute or two early for the appointment, and wasn't quite sure what to do. She eventually placed her notebook on the meeting area's table, and stood waiting, looking out the window. In the street below she saw a familiar figure, and she leaned forward on the rail to get a better look. As she did so she crossed one foot behind the other, tightening her calf muscles, making her legs look longer. She automatically tugged her hem down.

"Don't do that, that's the perfect inch."

Theresa turned around quickly, her hand to her cheek. "God, you startled me, I didn't hear you come in."

"I'm sorry," replied Madelyn, "I shouldn't sneak up." She stood next to Theresa, looking where the girl looked. "Isn't that Adam Cain, down there in the street? I wonder who he's with?"

Madelyn tapped her fingernails on the glass as if to get Adam's attention, but of course they were too high up, he couldn't hear a thing. She shook her head, a surprisingly soft smile on her face, and turned to Theresa.

"Come, my dear, make yourself comfortable and we can have a chat." Madelyn gestured for the girl to sit, then leaned down and quickly flicked away a button on Theresa's blouse. "There. Much better, don't you think?"

Madelyn sat in the other pod, curling her legs under her. She unzipped the bottom half of the long zip that slashed her skirt from hem to waist, revealing a stockinged leg and the smooth pale flesh of her upper thigh. She relaxed into the pod. "Ahh, that's more comfortable."

"Now, Theresa, tell me all about yourself. Tell me what excites you."

About the Author

A.A. Cain is an author of erotic tales living somewhere in suburban Australia. His work has been described as, "almost poetic; stories told by a crackling fire on a cold winter night, with a smooth whiskey in hand, listeners curled at your feet."

Cain's stories move from the floating world of city cafés and fashionable galleries, with contemporary men and women finding pleasure in familiar places, through to mysterious, mythical worlds populated with angels and astronauts, mermaids and men, and always, dark, seductive women.

www.ingramcontent.com/pod-product-compliance
Lightning Source LLC
Chambersburg PA
CBHW050533260626
47157CB00004B/1584